Victor was first to realize what had happened. 'Floris! Floris! Floris!' He ran at the row of four attackers, but one of them thrust his shield forward, meeting Victor head on. Victor rolled backwards, his nose pouring blood.

'Come on, we've got one of them,' the weasel shouted.

Victor let out a high-pitched cry, but before Bradley and Hunger could act, the attackers brought the patched door crashing back into place and held it with a wooden plank.

Though it seemed hopeless, there was a corner of space that Fearless squeezed through, her back bent, the ridges of wood scraping against it. Her back legs kicked furiously and she was through and into the night.

By the time Bradley and Victor had broken out, there was no sign of them and the swirling snow was already burying their tracks.

Also available by Tom Pow and published
by Random House Children's Books:

SCABBIT ISLE

'Exquisitely written . . . a short classic' *Literary Review*

'So well-written it makes most books look clumsy and heavy-footed in comparison' *Achuka*

'*Scabbit Isle* covers a great deal: bullying, bereavement and the effect of family breakup. It is not, however, an "issues" book. Pow has contained all of these reflections of modern life within a highly entertaining ghost story encasing social and familial disintegration centuries earlier . . . the main characters are well-drawn in this intelligently constructed debut novel. I shall be on the lookout for Pow's next book' *Books for Keeps*

'A powerful ghost story . . . enjoyable and engagingly streetwise' *Irish Times*

the pack

TOM POW

DEFINITIONS

THE PACK

A DEFINITIONS BOOK

0 099 47563 4

First published in Great Britain by Definitions,
an imprint of Random House Children's Books

This edition published 2004

3 5 7 9 10 8 6 4 2

Papers used by Random House Children's Books are natural, recyclable products made
from wood grown in sustainable forests. The manufacturing processes conform to the
environmental regulations of the country of origin.

Set in Sabon 11.5/17pt

Definitions are published by
Random House Children's Books,
61–63 Uxbridge Road, London W5 5SA,
a division of The Random House Group Ltd,
in Australia by Random House Australia (Pty) Ltd,
20 Alfred Street, Milsons Point, Sydney, NSW 2061, Australia,
in New Zealand by Random House New Zealand Ltd,
18 Poland Road, Glenfield, Auckland 10, New Zealand,
and in South Africa by Random House (Pty) Ltd,
Endulini, 5A Jubilee Road, Parktown 2193, South Africa

THE RANDOM HOUSE GROUP Limited Reg. No. 954009
www.kidsatrandomhouse.co.uk

A CIP catalogue record for this book is available from the British Library.

Printed and bound in Great Britain by
Cox & Wyman Ltd, Reading, Berkshire

CONTENTS

FOREWORD

'You measure the justice of society by how it treats its children.'

Pérez de Cuéllar, former UN Secretary-General

I first came across the extraordinary story of Ivan Mishukov, in an article concerning Russian street children, in the *Scotsman* in 2002. However, the story was first drawn to the attention of the world's press in 1998. Then, Ivan was a four-year-old boy who had become the leader of a pack of dogs.

Mistreated by his alcoholic father, Ivan had taken to the streets. After feeding stray dogs the surplus food he had begged, he was adopted by them as their leader. A subsequent article explained that, due to its economic meltdown, Russia had over one million homeless children, 50,000 of them in Moscow alone. The article painted a harsh world of broken homes, of curfews, of desperate policing measures, and of teenage Fagins offering protection to the younger children.

A section on *Cruelty and Neglect in Russian Orphanages* on the Human Rights Watch website described the manifest failures of a system to cope with its 'social orphans', the official name for abandoned children. A brutal world was catalogued there, where deprivation and systematic humiliation were commonplace.

But if Russia provided the first impetus for *The Pack*, it was not my sole focus. In recent years, many European countries, in a period of rapid economic change, have similarly failed to protect their children, as have, in different circumstances, governing agencies in Africa: the proliferation of child soldiers in parts of that continent is also documented at length on the Human Rights Watch website.

Closer to home, a headline in the *Independent*, 'THEY ARE NOT WILD ANIMALS. BUT THEY MUST BE TAMED', opened a discussion on the moral panic associated with the infamous cases of James Bulger, Stephen Lawrence and Damiola Taylor. The horror of each murder was compounded by revelations of an underworld in our cities where children roam unchecked, 'like wild dogs'.

2002 also saw the publication of *Savage Girls and Wild Boys: A History of Feral Children* by Michael

Newton. This book provided a deeper insight into the lives of children 'brought up by animals, growing up in the wilderness, or locked up for long years in solitary confinement'. The book opens with Ivan's story and the assertion that his case is not so extraordinary after all. Certainly, once its shock is absorbed, we can see many of its elements have a rich literary past: the brutality of the world Ivan wished to escape, for example, is prefigured in Maxim Gorky's *My Childhood*; while the fascination with the orphan can be seen throughout Dickens and the gentler nineteenth-century genre of 'waif stories'.

The Pack grew from such a coincidence of material. Its context was a constrained and brutalized world, one element of which, "The Dead Time", owes something to recent European upheavals, but also to Piers Brendon's riveting account of the economic, social and political catastrophes of the 1930's, *The Dark Valley*.

I wrote the first draft at speed while at Hawthornden Castle on a writing fellowship. I was surprised by the story's momentum and at the turns it was taking. When I was writing *Scabbit Isle*, I was not aware that what I was writing was a ghost story. Similarly, I was well through the writing of *The Pack* before I realized that I was writing an adventure story; that is, a story where characters and their relationships are tested in extreme – and exciting – situations. The writing of every story is a journey – or an adventure; however, I hope *The Pack* is a story that never completely loses contact with its roots in a real world where there are children abandoned by those who should protect them and who therefore must form other relationships to survive.

The Pack is dedicated to Ivan Mishukov – the one representing the many – and to Kilda and Talisker, German Shepherd and Golden Labrador, the dogs I knew best when I was writing the book. I'd also like to acknowledge the help of *The Hidden Life of Dogs* by Elizabeth Marshall Thomas, which of the dog books I read gave me most pleasure and helped me to understand Kilda and Talisker better.

I would like to acknowledge the support of a Hawthornden International Writing Fellowship. As I said, while at Hawthornden Castle, I wrote the first draft of *The Pack* at speed. To make a book of it has required a much longer process. For helping me to make the book what it is and for being, at all times, sympathetic to my ambitions, I'd like to thank my editors at Random House, Delia Huddy and Harriet Wilson.

Thank you to Greg, Rosa and David for a true experience of the wild no words can match. And lastly, if writing a book is a journey, thank you again Julie, Cameron and Jenny for taking it with me.

Tom Pow
Dumfries, January 2004

PROLOGUE

The engine screamed as the driver, both hands round the gear stick, forced the transport lorry up into third. Thick black smoke from his cigarette washed over one eye and he cursed.

Still, they did the job, these old monsters. Their wheels were almost as tall as a man and the capacity of each was like the hold of a small ship – all stacked with sacks of potatoes, onions, carrots; trays of oranges, peaches, limes, star fruit, artichokes, asparagus and fresh herbs: the finest the Compounds could grow.

The driver smiled – at least the jerking would have woken Stringer. Usually, when they arrived at the depot in the Invisible City, he found him moulded to a sack of potatoes, his machine gun pointing harmlessly at the empty sky.

He drew the last inhalation from his cigarette, unwound the window and threw out the butt. The rush of cold air chilled the sweat that had formed on his forehead and chest as he laboured in the giant greenhouses of Compound 16, helping to load the lorry.

He leaned his forearms over the wheel. No more changing gear from now till the depot: Route 3 stretched out before him, one of the five limbs of the star that held the city together. He had made so many trips, now he could almost drive it blindfold. Of course, they were still given warnings; particularly the new drivers – 'Be vigilant, your cargo is gold' and all that – but really there was no need. Not these days. Even at night – and the first flecks of darkness were already in the sky – the route was floodlit, clear as a runway.

Careering down the route, feeling that surge of power, still gave him pleasure. It had been so different in the Dead Time. For what, in your tiny world, did you have power over then? Perhaps only those you could terrorize into giving up some of their food for your own brats; while in the great world – the one you had put all your faith in – there was chaos.

Overnight, everything you had worked for and saved for had become worthless: all the gilt-edged documents you had signed with such a flourish became fit only for lighting fires. And they had been promises. Yes, promises! Route maps of your life – *Futures*

Guaranteed. Not only yours, but your parents' and your children's as well. But in the Dead Time, there was someone else writing everyone's script. Someone or something – a vague but ruinous power, indifferent to anyone's dreams. And there was no road back that you or anyone else could see, for your mind and your body were on the scrapheap too.

So, after the chaos of rioting and looting, had come a despair that couldn't be plumbed. The uprooted world entered a time when nothing improved, nothing seemed to grow, nothing was worth learning. Only the warlords prospered, as people aged, grew sick, died – and, while they were able, fought their corner.

Was it any surprise that they yearned for order? And that, when it came, with the Invisible City shining at its heart, the design felt God-given, natural, right? It had been soon after the Zones were established and the first Compounds started to produce that the driver had begun making deliveries to the Invisible City itself.

It had still been the Time of Reconstruction and he remembered the hollow-cheeked, shambling migrants who had lined the road as he drove into the city. The Compounds had taken the best land and turned most of them into farmers of dirt and of stone. Only a few could get by. Occasionally, one of the migrants had glanced up at his cabin and their eyes had met and he had seen, in spite of the hunger and the tiredness, a faint hope shining there, for what the city might deliver to them and to their scrawny children. And foolish though he thought it, hope then had its reasons. For in each of the crowded Zones, once or twice a week, one of these capacious lorries would stop and sacks of potatoes and rice be broken open and distributed. Oh, they had needed a gun then, all right. But just to calm the excitement down.

There, there, the gun said, *this handful of potatoes isn't worth your life*.

What amazed the driver was how accepting the Zones-folk became. Like the best-trained dogs, they would stand back in a talkative queue till the sacks were opened, the scales in place, and they were bidden forward. But those who came to rely on the handouts to get by were soon to get a rude awakening.

There was great discussion in the Compound canteen when the change in the original directive was announced. It had come, they were told in hushed tones, from the highest level. And it was clear that it had to do with the restructuring of the Zones beyond the Invisible City. The most powerful warlords – Red Dog, Black Fist, Jumplead, Footrot and Screel – were to be given control over a territory each. These territories were to be known as the Forbidden Territories and their purpose was to act as buffer zones between the Zones themselves and the Invisible City. It was merely a 'precautionary measure'.

There was no cause for offence – simply a recognition that envy could have a corrosive effect and it needed to be guarded against.

'Drive on,' they were told now. 'No matter what, drive on . . .'

He recalled those first trips – how, seeing the crowd gathered as usual, he had put his foot down on the pedal and his fist on the horn. They had scattered like pigeons. Sure, there were casualties at the start. How else would they learn? The massive treads of the tyres took a couple; the gun stuttered a few times to warn off the others. But again, it was remarkable how quickly the Zones-folk came to accept that this was the new arrangement; that their inventiveness and resilience were now going to be tested in different ways.

There was no getting away from it though – people were stupid. They must know by now that he was never going to stop; yet there they were in the cold, clustering at the ends of the roads which led into their Zone, staring up at his speeding lorry. What were they doing but underlining the misery of their lot? Though some faces seemed to shine with a threadbare awe at the vision of plenty rushing by.

'Crazies,' he said out loud and stepped on the accelerator harder.

He glanced at his watch. He'd made good time. Stringer and he might get a chance to spend some time in the Invisible City before heading back to the Compound. It was now that he realized what the others were always telling him: that it was a privilege, in such a time, to be a driver. Precious few people could move between the worlds of the Compounds, the Zones and the Invisible City. There were even inhabitants of the Invisible City who had sidled up to him in a bar and asked him what it was like in the world beyond its boundaries. Some of them even looked at him with longing in their eyes. *They* were really the stupid ones, those who couldn't seem to accept when they were well off.

And his wife – huh! It was like facing the Grand Inquisitor. What are they wearing? Do couples walk hand in hand? Are there children in the streets? And it was amazing, for while in the Zones the city seemed to be dying – rusting, putrefying, belching steam from broken vents – the Invisible City was constantly changing: new shops, coffee bars, businesses.

He felt his excitement growing. There might almost be time to go to that bar they went to last time; the one with all that steel and glass and the girls. He glanced in the mirror. Luckily, he'd shaved.

Up ahead, he noticed an old man had stepped out from the huddle of people at a road end. He appeared to be walking towards the middle of the route. The driver frowned. Once or twice he'd had a young man testing himself, showing off as if he were in a bull run, then flinging himself clear at the last possible moment. Love and how to win it survived the most desperate situations. But this was an old man; his reactions would be slow. Better, the driver had long ago decided, not to meet the person's eyes. Why give yourself nightmares, after all?

The old man never made it to the centre of the road, which was some kind of relief. It was the huge mud-guard that caught him and knocked him under. It was a blind spot for the driver, so all he felt was the gentlest of jolts – too satisfying in its way, like stepping on dog shit.

The driver smiled to himself – ahead the lights of the Invisible City burned brightly, and he knew the depot had a powerful hose.

PART ONE

THE ZONE

CHAPTER 1

THE OLD WOMAN

Bradley knew what he had to do. He had to listen. The Old Woman had said often enough, 'If you're not willing to sit and listen, be off with you, for I'm not going to waste my breath on ears that aren't open to a story.'

He saw Floris and Victor jerk their heads to attention, tired as they were from their day's begging, always having to look into people's cold faces with interest and despair, for no one gave anything to a blank or careless glance. Bradley himself squeezed and rubbed sleep from eyes that had spent the day squinting in the winter light through piles of rubbish – old shoes, broken computers, clocks, lamps, hairdryers – for anything of value or of use.

If you could latch onto the thread of a story, it would

pull you into its world, which was another world, though it might also be your world, but not quite, and you could for a time forget the hunger that was always working in the pit of your stomach, the cold at your back, the distant siren . . .

So when the Old Woman called for it, Bradley and the others looked up from their split trainers into her lined face with her bright amber eyes, and they gave themselves to whatever story she had. Seven feet tall she was now – it was the first of her miracles – and sometimes, telling a story, she would rise from the box she sat on and spread her arms out and, with the brazier glowing behind her, cast a shadow on the broken wall like some huge prehistoric bird, her fingers splayed like pinion feathers and her voice sounding hoarse as the *kraak-kraak* of the crows, which were one of the few birds Bradley knew. But then she would settle herself down like an old hen coorying down on her eggs. Her eyes would return from the great landscapes she had created, and fix on their upturned faces. There was a silence you could almost touch; before she'd lift a few strands of thick grey hair from her face and begin again.

'So, Thomas, oh, Thomas, what was he thinking of? He ignored all the good advice he'd been given, for he thought it wasn't for him. He crossed the little stream by its two stepping stones and took the path into the forest. It was the smell of cooking that talked to his stomach and he could see the smoke rising in the sky above the treetops' – and here the Old Woman's hand spiralled gently upwards – 'for this smell, oh, this smell was so delicious, it was the most delicious smell you could ever imagine, it was—'

'Sausages,' said Bradley.

'It was sausages indeed,' said the Old Woman, 'and the smell of the sausages drew Thomas on, till in the clearing he saw it, laid out on the grass, a cloth with plates of sausages, toasted marshmallows and nuts. Thomas looked about himself. He'd been told often enough never to cross the stream, never to touch the fairy food, but he was so hungry and there was no one about. He was so sure of that . . .'

Bradley looked across and saw Floris's blond head falling onto her shoulder, her eyes flickering open and shut, open and shut, and at Victor nodding slightly, his square face earnest and pale, willing the Old Woman to carry on, not to finish, though he sensed the end in sight; willing her not to bring them back to where they were, squatting on the hard earth round a rusting brazier. Three dogs dozed among them; one of them, black as coal with a silver chest, was so large no stranger would have dared to rouse it.

'Thomas bent down and reached out a hand' – to a plate that seemed to sit just before where the children sat – 'and he picked up one of the sausages; it was a lovely golden brown. He raised it to his lips – oh, it smelled so good – and he took one bite. One bite and his fate was sealed. They came at him from everywhere! They jumped on him from trees, out of rabbit holes, from behind rocks. They were so small and so quick he couldn't make out their faces or their forms, but they squealed with delight, their sharp teeth flashing, and they held Thomas and bound him and they took him under the green mound where they lived and where he would never ever be found.'

The Old Woman swept her eyes from one child to the other to make sure the lesson had been learned: stay within the world you know; to be inquisitive about another will lead you only to your death.

'*Never ever?*' said Floris.

'*Never ever,*' said the Old Woman, whose performance was not quite finished.

'What is the world made of?' she asked.

'Ashes,' the children replied.

'Ashes and dust,' she said and held out her hands to let one or the other blow from her huge flat palms, till there was no sign of it.

'All worlds,' she said. 'All worlds . . . But what cannot crumble, what cannot burn or be broken?'

'Stories,' the children replied.

'Stories,' she said. 'Now be gone and let an old woman get some sleep.'

From time to time, Bradley had watched bats go to sleep, pulling a long thin wing over themselves, and so it was with the Old Woman, who pulled a wing of her black cloak across herself and closed her eyes. The children rose then and left her without a word, the dogs – Hunger, Fearless and Shelter – padding behind them. Where the Old Woman finally stretched out herself – or if she ever did so – Bradley never found out, but if ever he passed her brazier at dawn, the only sign of her was the story turning in his own head; the next he'd see of her was on the street, pulling off another of her daily miracles.

In the basement where they lived, Victor and Floris curled into each other on their nest of blankets like dogs and were soon fast asleep. The dogs themselves settled around Bradley, their breathing chests lightly pushing into him.

A story, said Hunger.

'You've just had a story,' said Bradley and gave one of Hunger's ears a playful pull.

A story, said Hunger.

The dogs looked at him expectantly. They liked to hear the rising and the falling of his voice, not crisp with an order, but unwinding at the end of the day.

'All right,' said Bradley, 'you win,' and he told them one of the Old Woman's stories, one of their favourites.

As the dogs settled to listen, he imagined a time when they would take this story into the forests and into the mountains the Old Woman had told of. The tale then would seem as distant to them as the shards of his own memories. But every so often, he thought, an image or a simple rhythm, lodged in the creases of a pink ear, might return and connect them again with the Old Woman and with the boy Hunger had saved to become their leader.

CHAPTER 2

HUNGER

Floris coughed lightly. Bradley saw the puff of her breath in the cold air. She didn't wake herself, but Victor momentarily opened an eye and squinted at her. Hunger raised the long black wedge of his head, sniffed the air, glanced at Bradley and, assured all was well, returned it to the pile of rags they slept on.

Bradley was already awake. He pushed the blanket from him and eased himself from under Hunger's weight. The black dog liked to sleep so close to him, often his paws or his belly almost pinned Bradley to the ground.

The first cold light of day angled in the slats of the broken windows. One corner of the basement looked precious and warm – a box of old switches, plugs and circuits. Above it, an old shopping basket hung from the ceiling.

From his nest, Victor watched him. Beneath his blanket, his body began to coil and the muscles to tense, as his stomach thought for him. What put the glare in his eyes this morning more than another was not a question that concerned him. The sealed lips of the scars he carried on his arms and legs had been speaking to him again. They reminded him of how, in a time of scarcity, starving dogs had turned on him, driving him from a nearby Zone. He had sought brief refuge in the Forbidden Territories before Bradley found him. But he would not trust easily again. He and Floris were alone. And instinct told him Floris was weak and needed food.

Bradley had only begun to unwind the rope from its hook and to lower the basket, when Victor pounced. Using his knuckles as front paws, in an enclosed space Victor was fast as a cat. He lunged at Bradley's arm with his teeth and the rope spilled from his hand, the basket falling dully on the floor and its contents – the stale slices of bread, some withered carrots and an onion – tipping out.

Before either of them could react to this, a black shape the size of a small deer arced before Bradley's eyes. Victor took Hunger's paws full on the chest and fell backwards. Hunger pinned him to the ground, covering him like a black table. He bared his teeth and nipped Victor's neck to let him know how vulnerable he was. His steady growl became louder when Fearless and

Shelter padded over, thinking to clear up breakfast. Instead, they settled back on their haunches, prepared to wait calmly, as every morning, for Bradley to divide up whatever food they had.

It was then that Bradley became aware of Floris in the other corner. She was whimpering behind her blanket, her eyes wide with terror, seeing Hunger stretched out above Victor, hearing that menacing growl.

'Hunger,' said Bradley, 'enough.' Hunger knew Bradley's tone, as Bradley knew his. Hunger took a few steps back; Bradley took his snout in his hands and stared a moment into his black eyes – to let there be no mistake, he was back in charge.

Victor scrambled up and retreated beside Floris.

All the dogs, even Hunger, whined as Bradley pulled the basket up and secured the rope. Only then would he deal with Victor. He moved slowly – no sudden movements – Victor was closer to his dog's life than he was. The Old Woman had taught Bradley to walk straight, to clean himself, to think for tomorrow, just as Bradley was now teaching Victor. But still sometimes Victor forgot and slipped back into the habits he'd shared with the dogs he had lived among: he ran on all fours, he fouled himself where he stood; if there was food, he wanted it all now.

As Bradley crouched down before him, he heard Victor's breath rasping in fear and anger. Victor pushed

Floris behind him; there was no fight, whether with Bradley, Hunger or the whole pack of them, that he would not face to protect Floris. But still his eyes would not meet Bradley's. Instead, they darted nervously around the basement.

Once, Bradley would have reached out and grabbed a fistful of Victor's hair and forced him to meet his gaze; once, he would have added his bite to Hunger's.

'Victor . . . Victor . . .' Bradley put the flat of his hand out in front of Victor. If he wished to sink his teeth in, now was his chance. Victor cocked his head, then looked down. Bradley cuffed him, rocking him back on his heels, and for a moment Victor's eyes flared up at him. Bradley held his gaze steady and Victor again looked down.

Bradley reached his hand out again, but this time ran it over Victor's black spiky hair, remembering how, when they had found him – a stray from the Forbidden Territories – his hair was long and matted down his back, his legs and arms covered with bites. He would only allow Floris to get close to him then. She had poured some water from the can over a rag and dabbed at his wounds, no more scared of him than she would have been of a bird tipped from its nest. Or, more properly, a child. For, from the start, Floris had been able to see past the animal in Victor to the small, frightened boy he was. Still, in spite of Floris, in those early days and weeks he would squat awake all night, his eyes fearful and glowing like blue coals in the darkness.

Though Victor never spoke of it, Bradley imagined things were a lot worse beyond the territory Hunger, Fearless and Shelter mapped out for them. Certainly that was what the Old Woman believed; she was never done warning them to keep within the Zones, never to stray into the Forbidden Territories or to dream of the Invisible City, whose distant lights they could make out pooled in the dark sky.

'Victor is OK,' said Bradley. 'Victor is OK. Floris is OK. OK with Bradley, Hunger, Fearless and Shelter. One of us, Victor. One of us, Floris. We share.' Bradley opened his arms and passed them in a circle around Victor, Floris and Hunger, who had patiently tucked his head between his forelegs.

Victor stared back at Bradley through his tears. 'One of . . . one of . . .' He coughed out the words.

Just then, Floris began to smile. Shelter, the youngest of the dogs, was on her feet and snapping furiously at a sunlit column of dust stirred up by the commotion. With each snap, her paws left the ground and she took a little jump backwards. Victor, turning to see Floris smile, began to smile too; then Floris gave a light trill of a laugh. Victor stuttered out his own broken laugh and Bradley laughed when Hunger, Fearless and Shelter began baying along with a sound they couldn't imitate, but whose meaning was clear. For Hunger understood the big emotions well enough. He knew when a story was happening and when it had come to an end and he could communicate these things to the other dogs.

'Well,' Bradley said at last, 'come on, there's more to eat here than sunbeams.'

He let down the basket again and took out the bread, the carrots and the onion. 'The bread now,' he said. 'The carrots and the onion we'll give to the Old Woman. She'll turn them into soup for us.'

Bradley broke up the slices of stale bread and shared them with Victor, Floris and the dogs. Victor wanted to take his piece in his mouth straight from Bradley's fingers, but Bradley held it out of reach. Victor grabbed it and ran with it into a corner to eat on his own. Bradley unscrewed the top of the old gallon can they kept rainwater in and took three good gulps. He poured a little water into three bowls before passing the can to Floris.

The sky had been full of an icy rain and the can was heavier than usual. Floris tipped it up and, losing control, spilled the water down her chin and her neck. The Old Woman and Bradley never laughed at waste, but Floris gurgled her delight. Her eyes were blue – blue as the piece of worn glass that was her most precious possession. She could lie for hours simply turning it against the light. It was only the size of a large coin but, looking through it, Floris could see another world. It was the world she had come from and to which she would return. In it, she lived in a house made of glass, filled with light. Each evening there would be a fire and, before it, she would sit in her mother's lap and listen to story upon story.

Her favourite game with Victor was to imagine the glass had been lost and to search for it. The pair of them would turn over the sacks and old rags they slept on, becoming ever more agitated, till, 'Victor! Victor! Here it is!' And Floris would clutch the glass to her chest and trill her delight to Victor and promise never to let her dream of home out of her sight again.

'Tell me,' she said to Bradley. 'Tell me again the story of my name.'

'Later,' Bradley said. 'Tonight. If I don't start soon, we won't be eating tomorrow – and then you won't be smiling.'

CHAPTER 3

THE WAGER

Bradley left Victor and Floris with the dogs and climbed out into the cold sunlight. The building above their basement had been an old warehouse. It had been looted and torched in the Dead Time. Its façade still stood, buttressed by crumbling walls. At its top you could read, carved in sandstone with pride, WYLIE'S ENGINEERING WORKS. Every so often, scavengers poked among its burnt offerings for something to barter with. But the Pack had left them with nothing.

No passing stranger could have guessed that under the reinforced floor, the basement was still intact. A loose mesh of charred wood covered the entrance and Bradley, Victor and Floris always glanced around before entering or leaving. As for the dogs – well, stray dogs were everywhere.

At the end of their alley there was only one street to Main Street. From the doorways of empty shops, eyes watched Bradley pass. Even in his hooded sweatshirt, padded against the cold, he moved lightly on his feet; you could see he had an animal awareness of what lay just beyond his vision. The eyes let him pass because he seemed at home in this world; they knew there was nothing he could give them.

On Main Street it was still early, but the traders were about their business. They moved slowly in their shawls and heavy coats, laying out their wares on blankets, trestle tables or in the centres of old tyres.

One man laid out the contents of a small sack of potatoes. It must have passed through many hands to arrive here. He sat by them with his wife, who held one in her hands like a squirrel, rolling it beneath her nose, her eyes shut as if the smell of earth were her most powerful memory.

Another man sat picking the insignia from a pile of old army uniforms. They shone dully from the tin plate he put them in. Uniforms were highly valued for their warmth. But the truth was, anything was of value – the old coins, rusty nails, broken-up computers, plastic Mickey Mice. You had to have something to barter with to survive. And the tricky thing was, though everything was of value, you didn't know to whom; so you had to simply deal and trade and hope that sometime you would meet someone who had something you really wanted – food, matches, clothing – when you had something they wanted as badly – a padlock with the key still in it, a chain, a knife.

Unless you had nothing. Unless you were a beggar.

That was how Bradley had started out. Begging in a doorway all those years ago; before meeting the Old Woman, who had instructed him on the value of cast-off objects and quick wits. His first memories were of sitting cross-legged, his head tipped back, his hands out before him. That was how Victor and Floris would be, when he passed them later that day, though sometimes, for passers-by, Floris would lean back in the doorway and Victor would tilt his head towards her and emit a little whimper.

It was in a doorway that Hunger had found him and later brought Fearless and Shelter to him. He was much younger back then, so did well with the begging. Not well enough to fill his stomach, but well enough to share. So when Hunger poked his black nose into his doorway, his slack jaw showing his sharp white teeth, Bradley offered him a piece of bacon fat. It was enough for him to return and soon Bradley was making two piles of food scraps, one for himself and one for the dogs.

Hunger, Fearless and Shelter. He named them not because of anything he saw in them, but because of what was on his mind at the time. Though Fearless, black as Hunger, but smaller and more compact, did seem to possess courage beyond her size. Whereas Hunger's ears were always upright and alert, Fearless's flopped at half-mast; a sign of her recklessness. And Shelter, the youngest dog, her golden coat thicker than Fearless's, her snout blunter than the other dogs', less attuned to trouble, turned out to be the most placid of the three. She had become Floris's favourite.

And Bradley? Bradley Prince. 'Bradley's' was the name of the shop where he had been found begging – an old ironmonger's, filled only with rusted buckets and blunt nails. And Prince? Because the Old Woman claimed Bradley had been abandoned by a beautiful young girl – a princess, no less – who had pulled up in a curtained carriage and left him with a blanket and with a tear in her eye. Of this, Bradley had no recollection, but the Old Woman was full of stories – and it was a kind of story she was telling now.

Bradley marvelled, as he did each time, at how she could transform herself into this small, fragile-looking woman. She glanced his way and saw him coming, but gave no acknowledgement. And Bradley did not know her.

She had the three cups on the trestle table and was holding up a small red glass bead.

'Come on, ladies and gentlemen,' she shouted. 'Come and place a wager! Look, it's easy.'

She lifted the middle cup to show the red bead.

'Now watch the cups, please.' She swapped the middle cup with the one on the right and then with the one on the left. A small crowd had already left the nearby traders and gathered round. They would have the rest of the day to rummage through whatever was on offer. But entertainment, well, there was little of that around.

'So where's the bead now? Have a free shot, someone.'

Before a finger could be raised, a man in a brown uniform forced his way through the audience and pointed.

'There. That one.'

The Old Woman would have spotted the danger, just as Bradley had. She would recognize him as a henchman of one of the warlords from the Forbidden Territories. There was a badge with a head of a red dog sewn onto his right arm. But Bradley caught no flicker of fear in her voice and he knew she expected him to play his part too.

'Let's see, shall we? Absolutely right, sir!'

Bradley turned round and shared his amazement with the crowd.

'But watch again,' the Old Woman said and moved the cups again, this time slightly faster. 'Where is it now?'

The soldier wagged his finger again. There was a time

when the Zone had been infested with slithering, pointy creatures and this man, with his thin face and his wide-set eyes, reminded Bradley of one they had called a weasel. She lifted the cup and the bead winked in the sunlight. It was time for the soldier to take notice of Bradley. Bradley tapped his arm and beamed his delight and excitement. The weasel bared his teeth.

'And that's all your free ones, folks,' the Old Woman said in as light a voice as Bradley had heard her use. 'Time to place your bets.'

The Old Woman reached into one of her skirts and brought out a small paraffin hand-warmer. 'This is what you're playing for, sir. What are you going to put up?'

The weasel bared his teeth again and reached for the hand-warmer, as if it were already as good as his, but the Old Woman drew her hand back sharply and tucked it back under her skirts.

'And what are you putting up?' she asked again.

'This sack of vegetables.' He said it slowly, giving weight to each word.

'Show,' said the Old Woman. 'I'm not a fool.'

'That remains to be seen,' sneered the weasel, in what he imagined to be repartee. But he peeled down the sack until the vegetables sat in his arms: carrots sleek and red to their tips, golden onions, potatoes still tight in their skins.

There was a shared sound of indrawn breath.

'A sack – a whole sack of vegetables,' one woman sighed, jiggling her baby on her hip.

'Aye, a small one though,' a woman in a moth-eaten fur coat sniffed.

'But look at them, look at them, when did you last see . . .'

'Good prizes, each one,' a silver-haired gent spoke for them all.

'But you'll never get your hands on these, old woman,' the weasel sneered. 'Let's play.'

The Old Woman lifted one of the cups extravagantly high and brought it down slowly on the glass bead. 'Watch the cup,' she instructed, 'remember, watch the cup.'

She moved the cups around as slowly as before and took her hands away. The weasel was thinking, staring at the cup, but somewhere he had lost his nerve. His finger snaked out, then he withdrew it and tightened his grip round his vegetables.

There was nothing for it; Bradley would have to play the game. He pointed to his trainers as his stake – true, they were split, but the boy seemed to have bound them well with string and with winter coming on, another pair of shoes in the family would always be welcome. The Old Woman nodded assent and Bradley, biting one of his knuckles – a nice touch, the Old Woman would tell him later – pointed to one of the cups. The Old Woman raised it and there was the bead.

'Yes!' Bradley shouted and the crowd clapped.

'I knew it,' said the weasel.

'I knew it too,' a boy, who had wormed his way to the front, said for the benefit of the crowd.

'Aye, and me,' said his friend.

'We all bloody knew it!' a woman from the back shouted, and the crowd laughed as the weasel clenched his jaw, and the Old Woman meekly handed over the hand-warmer.

'Huh. So,' the weasel said. 'Again.'

'All right,' the Old Woman said, showing in her hand this time, briefly, an old brooch, a stone – amber as her eyes – in a swirl of silver. The weasel bared his teeth.

The Old Woman raised the cup higher than ever.

'Watch the bead.' And slowly she moved the cups around, though for a couple more circuits than before. Still, a small child could have followed the cup in question.

The weasel was excited now, on the balls of his feet, and the crowd with him.

'That one,' he said. 'That one.'

'You're sure? That's the one you want?' the Old Woman asked, gently, as if he were a small child.

He shook his head up and down furiously.

But no one was more excited than Bradley was. He nodded agreement and elbowed the man, as one fellow gambler to another to endorse his choice. The weasel turned briefly to him. His teeth were bared from ear to ear – it was as close to a grin as he had. The hand-warmer would have been nice for himself, these cold winter nights; but the brooch he could trade on – there was always someone looking for something to brighten up his wife's day; something shiny and useless to remind her of better times.

The Old Woman pulled her sleeve back – no trickery – and in the silence reached out to the cup. The weasel nodded firmly as she placed each of her fingers over it and raised it up.

Nothing.

The crowd gasped.

The weasel's thin shoulders slumped with the shock; long enough for the Old Woman to reach over and pull the sack from his hand.

'No, wait a minute. It's a set-up. Where's that boy?'

But Bradley was nowhere to be found. He had taken the sack of vegetables from the Old Woman and, as long as there was no trouble, he would soon have it back in the basement, safely waiting for the night's meal.

The weasel had other ideas. 'I've been tricked. Come on, someone must have seen it. Come on, it'll be you next.'

But it wouldn't be, because they had seen the Old Woman operate before. She was working, earning a living. Everyone had to do what she could to get by. The soldier was from the Forbidden Territories, which edged onto the Invisible City. That was the only place you could get vegetables like these, traded for solder perhaps, a bag of silvery tears melted down from old computer boards. It was the only way the apples and oranges, the carrots and potatoes that travelled through the Zones ever ended up back there.

The soldier – now a stranger – was rising to fury. 'My sack, you dirty old bag of mischief, where is my sack? If it's not in my hands within a minute, you'll be a sack of broken bones yourself.'

He was cursing the fact that he had come here on his own; cursing his own misplaced confidence.

Hunger and Bradley watched from the shadows of a doorway. Hunger padded from paw to paw, though only Bradley could have heard his growl. He held onto him loosely by one pointed ear.

The weasel threw the table over and advanced on the Old Woman. *Change*, Bradley thought, *go on – transform yourself; be what you are and envelop him in the span of your arms*. But the Old Woman held herself resolutely in check; this was a secret miracle she would only share with Bradley and the Pack.

'Now, Hunger.'

Three great bounds and Hunger was standing between the soldier and the Old Woman. The hackles stood up at the back of his neck like a brush and his growl rolled like gravel deep in his throat. He made a couple of warning lunges, his jaws snapping, teeth clicking. Instinctively, the soldier raised his hands to his throat and his face.

'All right, that's the way of it, is it?' he spat. 'That's how you play it round here. But remember, old woman, this isn't over – for you or for that boy.'

He turned and stomped off. Some in the crowd laughed as they turned and headed back to the traders. A warming thing excitement was – aye, and small victories too – but it wouldn't be long before they'd all be stamping in the cold again and blowing on their hands.

'Fuss over nothing,' one man said.

'Still, what I'd give for a hand-warmer now, eh?' said his companion. 'Here, lady, give's a hold of that baby!'

The Old Woman would give it a rest for a day or two; lie low at the sight of a uniform. She could afford to.

Bradley passed Victor and Floris huddled in a doorway. Victor bent his head down, but Bradley held the sack open and they both peered in, their eyes brightening.

'Tonight,' Bradley told them, 'we all eat like princes!'

CHAPTER 4

THE LAND OF WOLVES

The Old Woman stirred the thick vegetable soup, rocking the pot slightly on the brazier, sending sparks high into the sky. Floris watched them as if they were the most wonderful fireworks. Anything shiny and sparkly she loved.

Victor, though, never took his eyes from the pot.

The Old Woman tasted the soup with the wooden ladle that hung from her waist. 'Heaven,' she said, wrapping one of her layers of skirt round the handles and lifting the pot off and laying it on the ground before them. 'Here, use this bread in it till it cools.'

So the children ate. 'Slowly, slowly,' the Old Woman said. 'Now taste your carrots and your onion, they're in there too, so there's vegetables enough for nights to come.'

When they had almost had their fill, Bradley signalled the dogs in. And what a lapping and a slurping there was, till Hunger took the pot off and rolled it along the ground, working it with his snout.

'And now, the hand-warmer,' the Old Woman said, her hand raised in mock seriousness.

Bradley brought it out of his pocket. 'I was going to—'

'Aye, I'll bet you were,' she smiled. 'A good day, Bradley Prince. One of the good ones.'

'Yes, and it's not over yet,' Bradley said. 'There's still time for a story.'

'Oh, a story – Lord save us, another story,' she said.

'Yes, and *we* choose this time – Victor, Floris and me.'

'So, what's your story to be about then?'

'The dogs,' said Floris. 'Tell us about the dogs again!'

The Old Woman pulled an old box beneath her and rested her elbows on her thighs. She had worked her miracle again and when she craned forward, she could sweep her head between each of the children, her face sometimes in darkness, but for the amber spark of her eyes, and at others lit red by the burning brazier.

The story was for Floris first, so it was to the twin-headed body of Floris and Victor that she began to speak.

'Far from here, across the Forbidden Territories, beyond the Invisible City, there is a road that travels north. It passes between fields that are green with potatoes, with turnip heads and carrots; fields that have plump cattle and sheep nibbling on their juicy grass. Once these fields were for everyone – for the villages that are nearby and for the cities too. Now, as you know, very little passes the Invisible City, the city you must never see.

'The road travels north, till the farmland runs out and the road becomes a dirt track, dusty in the summer, muddy and impassable in winter. It goes on like this for mile upon mile, while tall firs thicken around it, and if you're lucky, a deer may cross before your eyes, silently, in a great bounding leap.' And here the Old Woman's hand curved before them. There was no other world now but the one unfolding before them. Victor's eyes glowed with the freedom and the space this story was conjuring in his mind.

'Or,' the Old Woman continued, 'you may see the fat shadow of an owl skim the tops of the forest; the tips of its huge firs a smoky blue. But you're not finished yet. For when the track runs out, there is a small path, trodden by rabbits and deer, that leads you through the darkness of the forest a little way, till you come to a wide lake shore.

'You have been so closed in by the firs for so long, the openness of the lake, the light of the water, the vastness of the sky – all make you feel as if you've lost some weight you've been carrying with you. And it's true, for it's time to rest.

'You take off whatever bundle you've been carrying and pick the early spring strawberries that grow there, each the size of the smallest glowing coal. They are so sweet, you roll them in your mouth, crush them with your tongue. Try one . . .'

The Old Woman passed her cupped hand between the three children. Bradley and Floris took a strawberry each and placed it in their mouths. Victor looked from one to the other and frowned.

'Go on, take one,' said the Old Woman.

'What is . . . a strawberry?' asked Victor.

'The sweetest, most delicious thing you can think of,' said the Old Woman, and Victor jabbed his hand into the Old Woman's palm and sucked in the imaginary strawberry from his fingertips. He closed his eyes briefly, the better to taste it, and Floris smiled at his seriousness.

'Enough,' the Old Woman said, 'it will be dark soon and you still have a way to go. To the left of a sandy cove you will see a bush arching over the water. The bush is covered with bright red berries, but you must not eat these, even though the strawberries may be white and green with unripeness and these berries say, *Try me, just one*, you must not. It is the purpose of this bush to tempt you.

'Lift a few of its branches up and you will find a small rowing boat. Yes' – she nodded – 'you would all fit in. Pull the boat from under the bush and get in. Take turns in rowing, because it is a big lake to cross. Save a handful of strawberries for the journey.

'You will be rowing quickly to escape the darkness; already the lake is fringed with black. There is a small island you must pass where two herons live, birds with long necks and sharp bills, like these . . .' The Old Woman snapped her fingers at each child in turn. But there was no need; they were all in the boat, watching the two herons, as they had often done before, spread their great wings and sail across the darkening sky.

'Where are you headed for?' she asked.

'The cabin,' they answered together.

'Yes, the small jetty by the cabin. And when you have landed there, you are in the Land of Wolves. But of course, we all know that the Land of Wolves does not exist any more.'

What did and did not exist – or had ever existed – beyond his particular Zone, the Pack and the Old Woman, Bradley could never be sure of. Nor whether the slivers of memory which surfaced in him were ones the Old Woman had implanted or were all that remained from a previous life, long forgotten.

'The story. The story,' said Floris.

'In the Land of Wolves, long ago, the wolves kept to themselves, as did the cabin people, though sometimes they sang to each other, when the moon was so beautiful and neither people nor wolves could stop praising it.

And the wolves would come close to the cabins and the people – the very few that were there – would put out some scraps for them and watch, just for the pleasure of seeing their silver coats, their bright yellow eyes and the way they flowed out of the forest and back again on silent feet.

'And so they lived together, not happily, not un-happily, but simply being people and being wolves. Till the Dead Time came . . .

'And in the worst of the Dead Time, when people had nothing to eat and the harshest winters to endure, the boldest of them – or the most desperate – left the cities and came north to see what they could find. And they found the wolves and they found cabins they could stay in, while they trapped and skinned wolves that had lost their fear of people. And so successful were they at what they did that soon there were very few wolves left in this huge area; and those male wolves, which bayed at the moon with such sorrow now, had no females with which to mate.

'And that's when the wolves began to travel. In winter they moved in their tireless flowing strides across the frozen lake, down the path, through the forest by the road and across the farmland, till they came – only the strongest and the wiliest – at long last to the edge of the Zones, where people lived in tents and boxes and places made of mud and where stray dogs lived, scavenging among its refuse. And there they found their mates.

'One magnificent wolf, his shoulders three feet from the ground, as long as Bradley is tall, his eyes burning like candle flames, chose a bitch as black as coal, almost as big as himself, but with a heart in pain from being driven away from a family's love. No dogs were allowed in the Invisible City – or were welcome any-where else. And so the great wolf found her and both bayed their fierce joy beneath the moon and from their union—'

'Hunger was born,' said Floris.

'Hunger was born and was the best of both his parents. No dog has ever been as courageous, as intelli-gent or as loyal.'

These words, Victor was thinking. *What do these words mean?*

Hunger always seemed to know this was his moment. He sat up, attentive, waiting for Bradley to put his arm around his neck and hug him.

'And Fearless and Shelter too, they also have some wolf in them and, if you look deep and long into their eyes, you will see, reflected there, lakes, forests and stars.'

The children smiled.

'Now, what is the world made of?'

'Ashes. Du—'

'But what of the people who came to the Land of Wolves?' asked Bradley.

'Ah,' said the Old Woman. 'That, as you know, is another story. For it happens that if you eat certain animals that are not meant to be eaten – like the wolf – the spirit of these animals will rage within you, such that you will become a cage for them and then a partial home for them. So these settlers in the Land of Wolves who had sung their hunting songs as they roasted the stripped wolves over spits by the lakeside, by morning held their stomachs, as something inside them harried their own flesh, circling and stabbing. And at night they clutched at the howling in their heads that would only stop when they staggered out of their cabins and turned their worn faces to the moon.

'Some tried to return to the city, but they were shunned for their babbled horror stories. Others accepted their curse and took to a life in the forest. Half man, half wolf, they are at home in the worlds of neither, yet the darkness of the forest can at least cloak their shame.'

Beyond the brazier's glow, Bradley saw the wolf men circling in the shadows. They were slim and sinewy, their movements graceful. What was human and what wolf was a blur to him, but when they turned to the light, Bradley saw their sharp ears twitch, as their human lips told him of a loneliness that made him shiver.

The Old Woman was holding out her palms. 'Now. What is the world made of?'

'Ashes. Dust.'

And the first few flakes of snow fell, dampening what ashes and dust the breeze did not blow away. She wiped her hands on her skirts.

'Ashes and dust . . . All worlds . . . All worlds . . . But what cannot crumble, what cannot burn or be broken?'

'Stories.'

'Stories. Now be gone and let an old woman get some sleep.'

CHAPTER 5

THE ATTACK

Floris's cough was getting worse. An early winter had taken root in her chest and in the night she rasped herself awake. Victor was so used to it by now, he slept through it, though at times, in his sleep, when she coughed he cuddled himself against her.

Even in the darkness, Floris could see how Victor's face changed in sleep, how the tension that kept his jaw tight all day left him – and the harsh years of experience fell from him. She slipped out of his arm and came over to where Bradley was lying. Hunger watched her. She stifled another cough and touched Bradley's shoulder.

'You said you'd tell my story tonight,' she whispered.

'We had a story,' Bradley said.

'Yes, but you said *my* story. You said.' Tears stood in the rims of her eyes.

'Yes, all right. But there's not much to tell.'

'I know, but it's mine.'

'All right.'

Floris smiled and sat back on her heels.

'Your name is Floris because you were born beside a florist's shop.'

'What is a florist's shop?'

Bradley knew all the questions Floris would ask, as she knew all his answers. It made no difference. There was not much to tell, but this was one way to make it more.

'A shop where they sell flowers.'

'Tell me, what flowers did they sell in my shop?'

'There were huge vases of roses, the size of both my fists – yellow, red and pink – all the colours you could think of. And lilies – lilies white as snow, the size of trumpets.'

Fearless had found Floris in the doorway of a shop with a missing T. It was long past the time when anyone in the Zones bought flowers – you couldn't live on flowers, after all – and the shop now pretended to be a butcher's. It sold the occasional pig's trotter, a cow's tail that could be boiled for soup. The butcher let Floris sit in the doorway during the day. 'Brings in the custom,' he used to say. For a while, at any rate, beneath the grime, you could still tell she was a pretty child. 'Though looks still need fed,' he'd said. It was a common expression of hard-nosed sympathy for those who had struggled to keep a child.

Floris would find scraps of meat for Fearless and one day Fearless brought her to the basement. It was warmer than the butcher's doorway and she had not wanted to leave. Bradley, seeing what she was like with the dogs – down on her knees, her earnest blue eyes brightening – had pointed her to a corner where she could sleep.

'Who bought the flowers?' Floris asked and put her fist to her mouth to stifle a cough. Her shoulders shook with it.

'People bought them for their houses,' said Bradley, 'or to give to people.'

'Who? Who do you give flowers to?'

'Anyone you like.'

'I'd like someone – to give me – flowers. Flowers – to me and Victor.' There was a shiver in her voice. Bradley stroked the curved knuckles of her spine and she crept back to her nest with Victor.

There had been times when the Old Woman had tried to give Victor the gift of a story of his own too. But Victor had turned from her gaze and become agitated. He put his hands over his ears and rocked back and forth: 'No-o-o-o-o-o,' till Floris had held him and calmed him.

No matter how circuitous the route, there was no

way Victor would revisit his past, and the Old Woman saw that his story, whatever it had been and would come to be, was indivisible from the one he and Floris would make together.

Hunger's eyes flamed in the night. They were fixed on Bradley – wide and alert.

'What is it, Hunger?'

Hunger turned his head from Bradley. His ears leaned forward into the darkness, as he sniffed far into the distance.

'It's the wind. Only the wind . . .' It whispered through the slats in the windows, between the camouflage of the door. Bradley rubbed Hunger's silver chest, but he would not be calmed. The Pack all shared an instinct for danger; they could all live on very little, they could all make decisions that appeared cruel if necessary and they could all cover ground quickly and silently – as cats. But Hunger could do more. In a dangerous time, he could sift patiently through the air, discarding the common dangers for ones that threatened Bradley and the Pack. He had a sense of something now – only the wind, perhaps, but when dawn came angling through the cracks, Bradley was unslept and all the next day he could never shift the feeling that something lay in wait for them over which he had no control. It could simply be a change in the weather or something more calamitous. In these uncertain times, one could never be sure which.

That night, a snowfall muffled footsteps. Warning smells carried in the air were swept off track, swirled above the rooftops. Hunger padded the basement, confused. Fearless and Shelter too took a long time to settle. It seemed Victor had gone back to his old ways, squatting on his blanket, his head swivelling like an owl's, his eyes burning through layers of darkness.

He had almost convinced himself of safety, when he heard too late, as Hunger did, the crush of snow as a foot steadied itself. A moment later, a club splintered the window slats and the camouflage door was wrenched open.

The torches soon followed. Flaming rags wrapped around sticks. The flames drove the dogs wild, but they angered as much as scared them. They stood at the doorway, their hackles up, as four shadowy figures advanced and retreated, banging dustbin lids. Victor meanwhile yowled and stamped and half rolled on the flames.

Hunger and Fearless snarled and snapped, baring their perfect rows of teeth. The attackers showed no inclination to try their luck – none of them appeared to be much bigger than Bradley was himself – but still they stood their ground, each banged lid goading a growl from the dogs.

'Come any further and my dogs'll tear you to pieces,' Bradley called. 'I mean it.'

'Come any further. I don't think so.'

'Into your stink hole.'

'Smell it from here. Piss-the-beds.'

'No thank you very much . . .'

'Cheesy-feets.'

'Good one!'

'So what do you want?' Bradley shouted above the banging.

'What do we want? What do we want? What do we want?' echoed the sing-song voices.

But in the commotion – the flare of flames and the darkness – they could not see what was happening in the back of the basement. The weasel man had slipped in through two ripped-out slats and grabbed Floris, who had been cowering, limp with terror. He had shoved her back through the slats and was almost free himself. He was pulling his legs through, when Fearless spotted him. She bounded over and leaped up, fastening her teeth round part of the weasel's bare calf. The weasel howled in pain and kicked at Fearless's head with his other foot. Fearless fell to the ground, but even in the darkness you could see the spill of blood on the concrete floor and the weasel could be heard outside: 'Bastard dog! Bastard dog! I'm going to poison the lot of them!'

Victor was first to realize what had happened. 'Floris!

Floris! Floris!' He ran at the row of four attackers, but one of them thrust his shield forward, meeting Victor head on. Victor rolled backwards, his nose pouring blood.

'Come on, we've got one of them,' the weasel shouted.

Victor let out a high-pitched cry, but before Bradley and Hunger could act, the attackers brought the patched door crashing back into place and held it with a wooden plank.

Though it seemed hopeless, there was a corner of space that Fearless squeezed through, her back bent, the ridges of wood scraping against it. Her back legs kicked furiously and she was through and into the night.

By the time Bradley and Victor had broken out, there was no sign of them and the swirling snow was already burying their tracks. Still, Bradley walked out to be clear of the smoke fumes, to escape the claustrophobia, to think clearly what he should do. Hunger's shoulder leaned into him, and the dog watched him with his keen, yellow eyes.

'No,' Bradley told him, 'not tonight. It's too dangerous tracking at night. Tomorrow the trail will still be fresh.'

But Bradley knew it was Victor he needed to speak to most.

He found him, snuffling around Floris's bedding, her

blue-glass in his hand. A steady whine came from him. Bradley noted that he had wet himself.

'Victor,' he said, 'Victor, you must listen.' Victor looked at him with huge, wild eyes. In the shadows the dark streaks of blood he had spread across his face looked black. 'Victor, I know where they've taken Floris and I know why. It's me the weasel man wants. Me and the Old Woman, but she's too smart for him.'

Victor spoke haltingly, each syllable on the edge of a growl. 'You say Floris is OK. You say Victor is OK. You say—'

'I know.'

'Floris is not OK. Floris is not here. And Victor not OK. No Floris, Victor not OK.'

Bradley took hold of Victor's hair and lifted his face to his own. 'I do know, Victor, I do know. But tomorrow Hunger and I will start on her trail. Fearless already has. We'll get Floris back. Tomorrow, OK?'

And Bradley thought he had calmed Victor down, convinced him that all would be OK, for Victor fell against him and let Bradley stroke his head and ease him down onto the bedding he had shared with Floris, till Victor seemed to fall asleep, though Floris would have spotted the line of his jaw still set, his eyes working below their closed lids.

Exhaustion carried Bradley far off below the surface of sleep, where he usually floated through the night.

Lost in the depths, he was not aware of one who could cover ground quickly and silently as a cat. But they had all developed similar habits to survive, so it came as little shock to find in the morning when a full sun dawned that Victor was gone and that the Old Woman stood, filling the doorway.

The Old Woman entered, stamping the snow from her feet. Bradley saw the white world glimmer beyond her.

From her night place, wherever it was, she had caught a glimpse of Victor, like a ghost, bent low, his hands at times brushing the ground, keening softly to himself, as he followed Floris's trail.

'I should have known,' Bradley said. 'Night holds no terrors for Victor.' He remembered from the night before how the blue glare had returned to his eyes, the nocturnal eyes of a cat or a dog. Once Bradley too had had that power.

'Knowing would have made no difference,' the Old Woman said. 'Floris is all that keeps Victor in the human world; the only tenderness he allows in his heart. He will do all he can to find her and, if he doesn't, yes, he will die as a dog, one that can't even return to the pack. No, nothing you could have done would have stopped him.'

Bradley recognized the truth of what the Old Woman said. He recognized too that what burned so brightly in

Victor, about whom he knew so very little, was his desire to be something different from what he was. But Bradley also knew the shifting nature of the boundaries Victor had to cross to get there. And how necessary it was that Floris be with him on his journey.

Perhaps with Fearless he would be all right. Perhaps together they would know to come back for help. But then again, Bradley also knew, though his own eyes had lost some of their power, his ability to think things through had increased. And he could not see anything holding back Victor's or Fearless's anger. Bradley knew he had to set out after them as soon as possible.

'You mustn't do it,' the Old Woman said.

'What?'

'You mustn't go there.' How could it be, Bradley thought, that the woman who had filled the doorway so recently had shrunk so much? She was no different now from any of the other feeble old women who would not survive this winter.

'Why?'

'Because if you cross the boundaries, there is danger everywhere. Danger that you'll never return. Did you not listen to my stories?'

'Every one. But there is nothing else I can do,' Bradley told her.

'But there is, you can stay here . . . you can—'

'I can't . . . do nothing.'

'Then you will need all your wits and all your courage. And luck – a good seasoning of luck.'

'I'll take Hunger with me. Shelter will stay here and fend for herself.'

'I will look out for her,' the Old Woman sighed.

'Good. She will be a good guard dog for you to have around in case the weasel boys come back for you.'

Bradley wanted to be gone now, for he was beginning to feel new and different terrors. Not the ones he would have to face on the trail of Floris, Victor and Fearless, but the unaccustomed terror he felt deep in his stomach, when he looked at the Old Woman's strong but tired face, her soft eyes, and heard the voice he had so often lost himself in. It was the thought of leaving her. It was a desperate need to keep something to hold onto – something he could take with him – that made him ask, 'Old Woman, what is your name?'

The Old Woman pulled off her headscarf and shook it. Her hair curtained her face, till she swept a hand through it.

'One last story,' she said.

'I was a teacher before the Dead Time. Yes, of children your age. Children whom no one else wanted to teach. I taught reading and writing. I taught that the world was a beautiful place and that the world was for everyone. And reading and writing, these were the tools to get you what you wanted – they were the foundations on which everything was built. Reading could take you into the worlds of the past or into the future. With writing you could create your own world or leave your own world for someone to discover – a world that would live for ever. For nothing lives for ever – only stories.'

'Ashes and dust,' said Bradley.

'Ashes and dust. That's what I've learned.' The Old Woman, Bradley noticed, had folded her scarf up into an oblong doll. She kneaded and she stroked it as she talked.

'I was a mother too many years ago and a grand-mother. There was a place I liked to go with the children – a cabin far in the north—'

'Where wolves once lived?'

'Where wolves once lived. When the Dead Time came and they shut my school, that's where I wanted to go. I arranged with my daughter to meet me at the heart of the Invisible City and to bring the grandchildren. I'd bargained with someone for an old truck that wouldn't arouse suspicion.

'Things in the Invisible City weren't much better than here in those days. Vigilante groups had established strict curfews to keep the lid on the looting and the law-lessness. Up ahead of our truck, I saw a barrier. It was a checkpoint and I knew they wouldn't allow us to pass. I put my foot down and swerved to get round them.

'The wheels of the truck went over some loose bricks

or something. The truck went over on its side and I was thrown clear. But just before I was, I heard the shots that ignited the petrol tank. The truck flared up. No one stood a chance . . .'

The Old Woman seemed to be folding herself into herself, like the head-kerchief she squeezed in her hands.

'And you?'

'I don't know. Someone found me unconscious and spirited me away. I was nursed back to this. But I knew then that, to survive, I'd have to lose everything I'd known – how to read, to write, what I'd been, my name. All of that was over . . .'

'Bradley' – the Old Woman reached out and gripped his forearm – 'remember, I've told you the stories you need to survive. Remember them. And better for you . . . if you don't come back.'

'Your name?' Bradley asked.

'Bridget,' the Old Woman replied. And then, with the faintest hint of pride, as if she were blowing dust from an old family relic, 'Mrs Bridget Newton.'

PART TWO

THE FORBIDDEN TERRITORIES

CHAPTER 6

CAPTURE

Bradley carried a small black backpack with a couple of slices of bread and a ham bone the Old Woman had brought out from her skirts and pressed on him. He took one brief look round at her, framed in the doorway, Shelter at her side. She seemed about to wave, but only brushed something – a snowflake perhaps – from her eye.

The snow was thick and before leaving Bradley had bound more rags round his feet for warmth. The laces of his trainers strained to close.

Hunger knew where they were going. He loped along before Bradley, his nose at times deep in the snow as he tracked Victor and Fearless. Every so often he would stop and turn to Bradley with a white nose to reassure him they were on the trail. Bradley nodded to him and waved him on.

They followed down Main Street, eerily deserted in the early morning, till they came to a broad square. In the middle of the square the snow was piled high on the neck of a broken statue. The square was the centre of a crossroads. To cross this road was to enter the Forbidden Territories. Hunger looked at Bradley: *Is this what you want?*

'Come on, Hunger,' said Bradley. 'We've no choice.'

At first, the Forbidden Territories seemed no different from the Zones: the same derelict buildings, the same braziers in the waste ground. They passed people wrapped in old blankets, stamping out the cold. Then they saw the first flag hanging from a street window. A black fist on a frayed white background – a sign to all from the warlord, Black Fist, that this territory was under his control. On one giant banner the fist appeared to punch a hole in a block of tenements.

Bradley and Hunger pressed themselves into a doorway. Four children appeared, dragging a sled. On it stood two others, their heads back, whooping. One of these wore a red blanket, which trailed on the ground behind him. The other began to point to an old man, scurrying up the opposite side of the street.

'Faster! Faster!' he shouted. 'Come on, Rudolph, you're for the knacker's yard, you.'

Rudolph turned round. 'Get stuffed, elf.'

'Come on,' Santa screamed above them both, 'he's getting away!'

The old man slipped and fell into the gutter.

'Got you!' said Santa, as elf and the sled-pullers surrounded him. 'Now, what you got for Black Fist's Christmas?'

The old man was pushing himself to his feet, when Rudolph put out a foot and sent him face down into the snow again. The children brayed.

'Right, let the old boy up now,' said Santa. 'He wants to show us what he's got.'

The old man rose slowly to his feet, then held his coat open, to show he had nothing for them.

'Pah!' said elf. 'Disappointing, old man.' Then he reached for the old man's belt and whipped it out. The old man's trousers slipped down around his ankles. The children cackled and hooted and pointed.

'Come on,' Bradley whispered, 'let's go now.'

They edged along the bannered streets, pushing themselves into the shadows whenever they heard a whoop or saw a gang cross a road in the distance. The last of the Black Fist flags were ripped or crossed with red. Then the markings began to show they had entered the territory of Red Dog.

And it was soon after these appeared that Hunger found her – Fearless – lying under a light covering of snow. She was already stiff and the cold had frozen up the head wound that had killed her. Her teeth were still bared with the rage with which she had thrown herself at Floris's kidnappers. A reckless black ear fell across one of her eyes.

Bradley reached out and eased the mouth flap down over her gleaming teeth and closed her bulging eyes. Fearless to the end. Hunger circled her, sniffing at her, a low whine singing in his throat. He lifted his head to the cold winter sun. Bradley knew what he was about to do and put his hands round his snout to quell the warring howl.

'No, Hunger, not now.'

Hunger's eyes, black as coal, were fixed on him. *I want to be before those who did this.*

'I know, Hunger,' said Bradley. 'But remember – Floris and Victor. We need to find them first.'

Bradley lifted Fearless up and carried her into a derelict shell of a building. He could not bury her, so he covered her with rubble and bricks. Whatever happened to her carcass, she was always more than it was. And now she too was a story.

'Victor,' Bradley said. Hunger turned from Fearless's grave, back into the street. They had to move quickly, for Bradley knew that Victor's tactics would be no different from Fearless's. He too might already be lying up ahead under a snow shroud.

* * *

Hunger moved with purpose through the rest of that day's afternoon, rarely lifting his nose from the snow. It dawned on Bradley that it was not simply the hunt that gave Hunger such sure intent, but deep knowledge of streets he had already mapped with his scent. For of course no Zone could contain his appetite for space. Deep within him, he carried the imprint of an endless forest. And Bradley wondered whether, like him, Hunger was tormented by the shards of distant memory – the slant of sunlight through the trees, the sharp tang of home.

They passed five men fighting over a coat. Two of them took an interest in the black dog and the stranger. They let go of the tails of the coat, letting the other three fall, cursing, into the snow.

'Hey, sonny, where are you going, eh? Come here, come on here.'

Hunger turned. His head was lowered, his hackles up, his teeth bared. Red Dog's lieutenant had talked of the fierceness of this dog, and the boy observing now from the street corner had thought he was exaggerating to save face – 'An old woman and a dog!' Red Dog had bellowed at him – but now he could see for himself the seriousness of the beast's intent. He left his post and ran off to report.

'All right, all right . . .' one of the men was whining. 'Only trying to be friendly.'

Hunger sank his nose into the snow and carried on, but he stopped more frequently now and glanced back at Bradley. Bradley nodded at him. Both of them knew they had been crossing and re-crossing the same territory: somewhere in the territory of Red Dog, they would find Victor and Floris.

But not today. Hunger had come to an old gutter running beneath the snow. The trail had gone cold and it was rapidly getting dark. At street level the only light guiding them now was coming from the snow, though the sky was lit by the constellations of the Invisible City.

I can go on. I can go on as long as my anger lasts.

'Tomorrow, Hunger,' said Bradley. 'Tomorrow we'll find them.'

They found a derelict building and settled down for the night. Bradley covered himself with an old pile of newspapers and Hunger pressed against him. Bradley opened his backpack and broke some of the bread between them and pulled some ham off the bone.

He spread his hand deep in Hunger's silver chest and soon was fast asleep.

'Bradley, good heavens, look at the time! If you're not careful you'll miss breakfast.'

Margaret opens the curtains and Bradley turns from the sunlight filling the room. He lies under the blankets – the blankets upon blankets – oh, the luxurious weight of them, the dog-warmth of them.

He gets up and stretches. He looks out of the window. The house is almost surrounded by trees. It is May and they are tall and full through the glen. A couple of woodpigeons burst from their tops in short frenetic flights.

Bradley's clothes are laid out for him – even in May, there is a soft, warm jersey for him, should he want it. He dresses quickly – a white shirt, with not a spot of dirt on it, and a pair of black woollen trousers – and goes along the corridor and down the winding staircase.

In the breakfast room, a fire burns low in the grate. There is hot porridge waiting and a plate of bacon and hot slices of toast.

'Good morning, Bradley,' says his mother. She wears a blue dress the colour of a summer sky. She has a complexion like cream, with almond eyes, blue as cut glass.

'Good morning, Mother,' says Bradley.

'Some porridge?' his mother suggests. But for a minute or so, Bradley just wants to look at her, to take in her softly tumbling hair, her kind face, her gentle hands, so that he will have them with him always; until she gives a trill of laughter and plants a kiss on his forehead.

'Oh, Bradley,' she says.

The table is set for another – Bradley's sister – and

when she arrives, her face is troubled. She bites on her lower lip as she greets Bradley and their mother.

'Oh, Mother,' she says, and there is a heaviness in the way she says it.

'Now, Chloe,' says their mother, 'you've not to worry about me – or about Bradley.'

Bradley notices then how alike mother and daughter are. They could almost be twins – the same blue eyes, the same elegant hands.

'What is there to worry about?' Bradley asks. 'Whatever it is, can't Father take care of it?'

They both turn on him their sad eyes. 'Bradley,' they say together, 'don't you realize yet, Father is dead . . .'

'How did he die?' It seems odd to Bradley how calm he is, asking the question, while seeing so clearly his father's face – the determined set of his jaw, his blind white eyes.

'Did no one tell you, Bradley?' his mother asks.

'No,' Bradley replies. 'Tell me.'

'Well, as you know,' his mother begins, 'your father was a very rich man. He owned factories throughout the land.'

'What did he make in his factories?'

'He made thick woollen cloth, silly – the warmest of its kind – and it went throughout the world, mostly to children. They loved its softness, because it never chafed them or cut into them. That is why you have never known a winter's cold, my darling.'

'So what happened?'

'He was testing a new fabric, far in the north on the ice floes; he always took a real, personal interest in the business. He wanted to make sure a new fabric did what he would claim for it – *Keeps You Warm, WHEREVER YOU ARE!*

'His factory ship looked like a whaling ship, sharp-prowed, broad in the beam. That was where the huge looms were located and the weavers worked, happed up in fingerless gloves and hats and scarves. For weeks they had been weaving and testing, weaving and testing. Your father held each new piece of cloth against his cheek and against the soft inside of his arm to check for softness. It was a test the cloth had to pass before it passed any other. If it failed, he might ask for four more angora threads in the weft, a bit of chinchilla in the woof.

'But the real test came on the ice, the coldest place your father could think to go. How could a blind man walk on frozen floes of ice? Yes, it was a question that was often asked. But what he lost in sight, he more than made up for in his hearing. The tiniest creak of the ice told him its thickness and where there was a weakness. The gentlest slap of water on the broken edge of ice told him the mass and dimensions he must cross.

'As you can imagine, at the testing time, the crew and the weavers all left their posts and leaned over the side of the ship to watch a blind man skipping across a jigsaw of ice. And all the time, remember, he would be calibrating the degree of warmth held in a leg, in a cuff, in each of his ten fingers.

'When he lost his footing on a particularly treacherous block of ice, the weavers and sailors at first took him to be dancing. They applauded his jig. Chaplin had never been funnier – or risked more to be funny. How these men loved your father.

'They cheered when he called out to them, laughed themselves hoarse as, limb by limb, he disappeared over an edge of ice. They waited in the silence for him to reappear on the other side. He was a man in whom one never lost faith.

'But to be brief, dear Bradley, your father fell into the freezing waters and drowned. Of course, he wasn't aware of the waters being freezing – the fabric worked, no doubt about that. Yes, your father drowned in a cold blue light but with a sweet, satisfied smile on his face. And, if you're looking for other comfort, it wasn't long before the weavers and sailors worked out what had happened and began to sing psalms and hymns, whose vibrations were the last sounds your father heard.'

'Dear Father,' says Chloe and begins to cry.

'Now, now, Chloe,' says her mother.

'But what's to happen? What's to happen to Bradley and me?'

'You'll be fine.'

But Bradley notices she doesn't say 'both' and he notices the worried glance she gives him.

'But I hate Uncle Vince!' screams Chloe.

Bradley knows it is important that he asks why, but the smell of the bacon is almost overpowering now. He just wants the conversation to end, so that Margaret will come in and serve him the bacon, because suddenly he realizes he has not eaten properly for days.

Hunger had smelled it too, the charcoal smell of burning meat. Bradley was as much animal as he was when hunger pangs struck. He brushed the newspapers from him – with the bones of a story the Old Woman had once told him – and took to the street.

Skewered on sticks thrust into the snow, each a house or so apart, there were three burnt fingers of meat. That things so small could smell so delicious! The street, in the grey early morning light, was deserted.

'Yes!' said Bradley.

Yes! said Hunger. They would grab the meat and take it back to the building to share.

Bradley's hands were on the third skewer when they fell on them. They poured from basements, from the black mouths of buildings; they seemed to rise from the snow itself. How many of them there were Bradley couldn't tell, but they fairly whooped with delight, their teeth flashing as they threw nets over him and Hunger. Hunger snapped through a few of the cords, till they bit too far into his mouth for even his back molars to reach.

Finally, exhausted with the struggle, Bradley and he lay panting on the ground.

Too late the Old Woman's voice came to him: 'Thomas, oh, Thomas, what had he been thinking of?'

Bradley could see clearly now, from his street-level view, that their attackers were all children, no older than he was, grubby and dressed in ragged clothes, though each wore a red badge of identity tied round his head or one of his arms. They were leaning down to him and grinning and howling. One pushed his face into the snow. They slapped each other on the hands and on their backs.

'That's him. That's the one. Got ya! Got ya!'

They fell silent and moved back from the net. Bradley heard boots crunching on the snow. One heavy step and then a lighter – someone with a limp. He looked up to see the weasel man smirking down on him.

'Works every time, that one. We knew you were around here somewhere. Just a case of flushing you out – right, boys?'

The boy soldiers chirruped agreement.

'Yes, well, like I say, we've been expecting you, little friend. We'd better go now; Red Dog's very keen to meet you.'

CHAPTER 7

RED DOG

The children threaded poles through the nets and carried Bradley and Hunger through the streets. Those not carrying danced beside them, poking fingers and sticks into their trophies. Two of the coat-fighters Bradley had met earlier, woken by the cold and the commotion from their doorway, showed a bleary-eyed interest. But the children snapped and spat at them, before laughing with each other.

Through the net, Bradley could see that they had been brought to a building with an impressive oak door. Above it was the motto, in chipped stone, MUTUAL INVESTMENT – FUTURES GUARANTEED. On either side hung two long banners, each with the profile of a red dog.

Bradley and Hunger were carried up a flight of stairs, their backs bumping on each step because the porters were so small. They were brought into a cavernous space and were dumped in the middle of its hard wooden floor.

The children withdrew to the sides and they were left alone, bruised and wild-eyed.

Helpless, said Hunger. *Pain*.

Bradley didn't know what to say. He pulled a hand from under him and pushed it into Hunger's chest. Their heartbeats knocked into each other.

As his eyes became accustomed to the thin electric light and the clumps of candles, Bradley could see they were in a huge hall that had been made by demolishing the walls dividing half a dozen rooms. He could make out the jagged arches. There was no furniture in the hall, apart from, at the far end, on a raised platform, a large swivel chair.

A door opened. The children began to whoop and bang. Hunger struggled to stand, but the more he struggled, the more he tied himself up. Bradley was terrified he would strangle himself.

'Hunger,' he said. 'Hunger.'

It was the first time Bradley had seen him with eyes on the verge of defeat. They were full of wildness, of course, and anger too, but fear was there, the fear of not being able to stand four-square to face whatever was going to happen. His red tongue was like a wound in the half-light.

The man who had entered was huge – and cursed with a grotesquely misshapen head. That much Bradley could see as he watched his back passing through the guard of honour. He seemed to be wearing a kind of frilly red gown. And he liked to play.

The game appeared to involve him breaking off from his stiff procession to his throne to cuff one of the children who had come too close. It was not a friendly cuff, but one which sent the child tumbling over and squealing with pain. The others laughed uproariously. In fact, it seemed to be the viciousness of the slap that added spice to the game. The bravest children went as close as they dared, skipping away with delight when he missed.

One child, though, pushed his luck. He had a shock of red hair and he glided out behind the man like a dancer, before imitating his walk for a few strides. The children tittered and the man swung with lightning speed. The blow caught the boy full on the side of his face. His feet briefly left the floor, as he hurtled sideways. The other children did not catch him, but stepped out the way to let him fall, clutching his head on the ground. His human crying did no more than amuse the others, who crowded round him making boo-hoo noises.

'You're getting slow, Skreech,' the giant called to him, blowing on his hand, as if it were a smoking gun. He then drew the same hand in a great arc across his chest and out before the company, till he brought it to rest at his side.

'My lords, ladies and gentlemen, *mutual investors all*,' he announced, 'may I introduce to you Red Dog – *once met, never forgotten; once crossed better you were never begotten.*'

He was the tallest man Bradley had ever seen, with a great barrel chest and a forehead that, when he frowned, seemed to push down on his brows like a helmet. The gravity of the ceremony demanded he frown most of the time. And yes, he was wearing a red frilly gown and a pearl necklace over a metal shirt. He stepped up to his throne and twirled once, sparking light through the hall, before he sat on it. The children cheered. And the helmet lifted briefly and he laughed, a high-pitched laugh that was cold as a draughty tunnel. The children laughed too at the nothing he was laughing at. An ice-storm of sharp little laughs.

Red Dog stopped laughing and in an instant there was silence, apart from Hunger's claws scraping the bare wooden floor.

'So-o-o, *Dog Boy*,' he sneered, 'you thought to pull a trick on one of Red Dog's lieutenants, eh?'

Bradley started to answer, to come out with some kind of impossible threat, but all he could manage were a couple of rasps. His chest felt badly bruised and cords cut across his lips.

'Cut him free and bring him before me,' ordered Red Dog. 'Leave the black creature to exhaust itself.'

Half a dozen children held onto the net, while the weasel cut through the cords. Bradley felt himself expanding, filling out the shape of himself. Hunger they secured even more tightly.

Bradley stood up shakily. Whatever he might have wanted to do, he couldn't have done it then; his legs trembled, his arms felt powerless. He took deep breaths to clear his chest.

The children, still all flashing teeth and bright eyes, poked him forward to face Red Dog. They pushed Bradley down till he was on his knees.

What had made the warlord's head appear so grotesque was a ginger wig, carelessly askew. Below it was a pair of red painted-on eyebrows, for Red Dog had none of his own. And the metal shirt turned out to be a chestful of medals. Bradley knew a little about medals, as the Old Woman had traded them for bets on a few occasions. Any medal worked as currency, but Bradley noticed in Red Dog's collection two for animal bravery and one that the Old Woman had told him they once gave for absolutely nothing with breakfast cereal.

'What a world that must have been,' Bradley had said to her.

'Well, it's long gone and it's never coming back. You remember that, if you want to survive this one.' Her fists had clenched, as if she were wringing something that would never quite dry out.

Still, no matter where they had come from, Red Dog was proud of all his medals. He thrust out his chest and shook it, making the medals jangle.

'See what kind of a dog you took on when you took on Red Dog, *Dog Boy*.'

Bradley breathed out, 'Where are they?' But the words only came as three short breaths.

'Sorry, didn't catch that, *Dog Boy*. Could you speak up a little please? Pretty please.'

'Where are they?'

'And who-oo-to-whit-to-woo would *they* be?' He turned his grinning face from one side of the hall to the other. Each side of soldier boys tried to out-clap the other.

'Floris and . . .' Bradley said.

'Floris,' said Red Dog. '*Flor-is*. Mmm. Now, would that be a lovely little girl with sparkly eyes?'

'Where is she?'

'Oh, not here, *Dog Boy*, not here.' Red Dog put his hands out, palms outwards, and called for a response.

'Not here, *Dog Boy*, not here,' the children echoed.

'I tell you, if you've—'

There was a kick in Bradley's back and his face hit the floor.

'Naughty. Not to threaten Red Dog.' It was the weasel's voice.

'Thank you, Laugh-tenant,' said Red Dog. '*Laugh*-tenant. Ooh, isn't that good? Don't you think so? I like names. What's your name, *Dog Boy*?'

My name is my story, Bradley thought. The name the Old Woman gave to him. His name was precious, secret, like Mrs Bridget Newton's was to her. Nor was he unhappy with *Dog Boy*, much though Red Dog sneered at it. It was dogs he lived amongst, after all, one of whom lay dead under rubble for caring for someone *he* as pack leader should have protected. Another lay behind him, cords cutting into his flesh – a dog that was like a brother to him. He had no shame in the name Dog Boy.

'Dog Boy,' Bradley answered. 'I have no other.'

Red Dog smiled, his helmet brow lifting back. 'Ah, Red Dog; Dog Boy.' He nodded. 'The Dead Time gave birth to many new names, did it not? Fair enough, Dog Boy, your Floris is not here.'

'Then, where . . . ?'

'We have shipped her on, shipped her out, have we not, my lovelies?'

The children cheered.

'Where? You'd better—'

Another foot to the back.

'Careful, now,' said the weasel.

'Oh, you are full of questions, aren't you?' said Red Dog, as Bradley pushed himself back onto his knees. 'All right, I'll tell you. She's gone to the Invisible City. There was a vacancy, you see.'

The children clapped delightedly.

'Someone had to go, didn't they, my lovelies?'

Red Dog's helmet came down and he circled the room with his eyes; first one way, then the other – then back, as if he were looking for one child in particular. The children were unnerved by this. They tried to avoid Red Dog's gaze by looking at the floor or to their sides.

'Oh, but next month' – he spoke slowly – 'next month . . . Oh, who's it going to be? I wonder. Oh, who-oo-to-whit-to-woo might hesitate, when Red Dog says, "Jump"? Who might say, "Oh, Red Dog, Red Dog, don't make me do that"? Oh, who-oo-to-wit-to-woo might it be who would draw Red Dog's attention to them? Could it be you, Blade?'

'No, Red Dog, never!'

'You, Skewer?'

'No, Red Dog, never!'

'It must be you then, Poker.'

'No, Red Dog, never!'

'But it *has* to be someone,' wheedled Red Dog. 'You can't all have *Futures Guaranteed*. Not in this cruel, cruel world. Oh, my boys, if you only knew the weight of responsibility . . .' Red Dog buried his head in his arms. In the silence they heard his terrible sobs. 'Has to be someone . . . Oh, boo-hoo, has to be . . . Oh, boo-hoo, this harsh, cruel world.'

The children held their breaths and waited.

Then Red Dog appeared to have the freshest thought. His head resurfaced and, when it did, his delighted eyes were fixed on Bradley.

'Unless . . .'

'Yes! Yes! Yes!' the hall broke out in a clamour of approval.

'Dog Boy! Dog Boy! Dog Boy!'

'Oh, we'll see. You see, Dog Boy, that other one, they wouldn't want him at all, sorry scrap of a thing that he is.'

'Victor,' Bradley said. 'Where is he?'

'Ah, Vic-tor, Vic-tor. Victor wasn't for telling us his name either, you know. So thank you for that. Poor Victor, he was terribly upset. Would you like to see him, Dog Boy? Come then.'

The weasel tugged at the neck of Bradley's jersey and he got stiffly to his feet. With children gripping his arms, he followed Red Dog through the door to the right of his throne and into a large square room.

This room was intact, a dim light spilling down from a broken chandelier, clumps of candles at each corner, and in two of the corners, two round cages, one ten feet across, the other considerably smaller. It was to the smaller cage that Bradley was led.

'Sssh,' Red Dog whispered, very showily rising onto tiptoe.

There was a bundle of rags on one side of the cage. Red Dog signalled to one of the children, who stood by with a cane. The child poked the cane through the bars and thrust it deep into the rag pile.

The pile erupted.

And there was Victor, his hands locked round the bars, snapping the cane with his teeth. His face was masked by a blue bruise, which had spread from his swollen nose across his cheekbones. From those markings his eyes glared so wildly, they seemed to be beyond seeing.

'Victor,' said Bradley. 'Victor.'

But Victor carried on growling and snapping, till Red Dog motioned to another two boys, one of whom thrashed at Victor's hands till he let go of the bars, while the other poked a cane into his stomach, lifting his shirt to show the red weals of a previous beating.

Howling in pain and anger, Victor retreated to the opposite side of the cage, where he licked his knuckles and curled his lip at his persecutors. Bradley noticed then that he wore a dog collar.

The children laughed at the sport and Bradley saw an invisible curtain come down in Victor's eyes.

'Victor. Victor. It's Bradley.'

Bradley remembered the Old Woman's words: 'Floris

is all that keeps Victor in the human world; the only tenderness he allows in his heart. If he doesn't find her, he will die as a dog.'

Seeing Victor's lack of recognition, the way he had crossed his cage on all fours, the wild yet beaten dog-eyes he turned on the whole company, Bradley feared the Old Woman would be proved right. For how long would Red Dog and his gang of boy soldiers be entertained by a creature, once the spirit had been beaten out of it?

Red Dog's verdict was already ominous: 'Oh, Victor, you're not much fun.'

Bradley looked across at the other cage, trying to see what he could make out there.

'Oh, the other cage, the other cage,' said Red Dog. 'The other cage, my beauty, is for you.'

The weasel opened the door and Bradley was thrown in.

'Bold Skreech, trusted Skreech, *bruised* Skreech, you will have the honour of tending to our guests. We'll see you tomorrow, Dog Boy. Sleep well,' and Red Dog and the company swept out.

A little later, they brought Hunger in. The weasel unlocked the door and the children slipped Hunger off his pole. He gave some rasping breaths and tried to right himself, but he was hopelessly trussed up now.

'You'd better get him out of that lot soon,' said the weasel, 'before he runs out of breath. Tomorrow's an important day for him. You want him fit.' He switched the light off and shut the door behind him. Skreech sat cross-legged in the corner in the candlelight, his head against the wall.

It was easy enough to feel for the knots, but it was hard in candlelight to see how they worked. And, with Hunger's struggles, they had tightened till the cords seemed to have fused.

Bradley worked with his nails and his teeth. A few knots came free, but with others Bradley had to chew his way through the cord itself. All this long time, Hunger lay still. His eyes followed Bradley.

'Trust me,' said Bradley and gave Hunger's head two good strokes, pulling his hand back from Hunger's forehead to the nape of his neck. *Trust*. If he had known the meaning of the word when they met, Hunger might have been differently named. But hunger was the place they had both started from.

Bradley heard Victor keening in his cage as he worked Hunger's knots. It was the softest, most mournful sound. Victor was as alone now as when Bradley had first found him, a stray from the Forbidden Territories, covered in bite marks, with 'Victor' the only word on his lips.

One last cord frayed and broke and Hunger was scrambling to his feet. Bradley pulled the remains of the net from him and Hunger shook himself, then circled himself, dabbing wounds with his tongue. He sat and licked his back legs and stretched the large thigh muscle where the cord had cut most deeply.

Bradley stroked the length of him and whispered softly into his ear. 'It's all right, boy. It's all right.'

Let me be, said Hunger. He squatted and he raised his head back and he began to sing, at first quite softly, then with a gathering power, till his singing came in great rolling howls.

With a scurry, Victor was on his haunches, his eyes piercing the gloom between the two cages. Then, his head thrust back, he answered and added to Hunger's call.

Something at the heart of their calls spoke to the child guard – the wildness of a spirit that would not surrender – so Skreech was half-hearted when he rattled his stick round the cages. But Hunger and Victor carried on in unison, till the weasel came in and threw a bucket of freezing water over each of them.

'Shut up, will you? Save your breath for tomorrow. You'll need it.'

Victor and Hunger shook themselves. Half the weasel's water had missed.

'Victor, we'll get Floris,' Bradley said.

Victor gave the smallest howl of assent.

Hunger lay down and rolled his body against Bradley's. Soon Bradley felt the heat of Hunger's blood coming through his fur and he imagined the earthy damp-dog smell of him was the smell of a deep, dark forest.

Whatever tomorrow may bring, he thought, let it come.

CHAPTER 8

A NEW CHAMPION

Shooting pains in his back woke Bradley. He twisted and lifted up his jersey to see the bruising. It was the sharp stair edges that had done the damage.

Skreech was slumped in his corner, his hands loose around his stick. A bruise marked the side of his face, most deeply where his jaw was swollen. Bradley scratched Hunger's ear and laid his head softly on the ground.

'Psst,' Bradley called. 'Psst.'

Skreech lifted his head from the wall. 'Mmm.'

'Looks sore, your face.'

Skreech looked at Bradley as if the question were crazy. 'What you want, Dog Boy?'

'Just saying . . .'

'Go to sleep, Dog Boy. Your dog's got the idea. He's going to need it.'

'Why? What's going to happen?'

'Big dog fight. Red Dog's got a champion – real killer. Your dog's going in with it.'

'And if Hunger wins?'

'Hunger, that his name?'

'If he wins?'

'Yeah, sure.'

'But if he does?'

'Then he'll be the new champion. That's how it works. But I tell you, no one lasts long with this animal.'

'Pity,' said Bradley. 'Hunger's a good dog. He's been a good friend to me. I'd hate to lose him.'

'*Friend* – huh, no one here cares about *friend*.'

'But aren't all these children who work for Red Dog your friends?'

'Don't make me laugh. They'd trade me for an apple if Red Dog told them to. And I'd do the same.'

There was a honed sharpness in Skreech's voice, yet he was younger than Bradley, slightly smaller and with more delicate features under the grime. Bradley felt he was forcing the voice to fit a shape he had in his mind.

'Why stay then?'

'You stupid, are you? What else is there to do?'

'I mean, what's in it for you?'

'My life. That's what's in it for me. I do what Red Dog says and I get food, I get shelter. He looks out for me – and for the rest, I take my chance with everyone else.'

'What kind of chance?'

'You heard him. The chance of being chosen.'

'I don't follow.'

'No, you don't follow nothing, seems to me, or you'd've stayed where you were.'

'Not a choice.'

'Pah. Chance of being chosen to go to the Invisible City.'

'What happens there?'

'You saying you've never heard the stories?'

'No, never.'

'Well, it's a place called The Mount they send you. They've got lots of children there, ones they picked up when they cleared up the Invisible City after the Dead Time. But still they need more. That's what Red Dog provides, a fresh batch . . .'

He stopped briefly and, not for the first time, glanced across nervously at the door into the great hall.

'No, no point in making friends here. When they go, they never get out. That I do know.'

'What do they do with them there?'

'Does it matter? None of us thinks about it much and we don't feel anything when someone's chosen, 'cos you know it could be you next time. Except it's not going to be me, it's going to be you. That's the only way you'll see Floris again.'

'Did you see her before they took her?'

'Yes. She was exhausted, but still crying and kicking. "They'll come for me," she was shouting. "They'll come for me." Red Dog loves these empty threats.'

'Well, we did.'

'Big deal. Look where it's got you.'

'It's not over yet.'

'Oh, but it is. Your dog dies today and you'll go to The Mount soon enough.'

'And Victor?'

'Oh yes, I was forgetting about him. Well, he's no good to The Mount, they're only interested in healthy types there, and soon Red Dog will get bored with him. I reckon they'll just turn him loose like a wounded bird. See how long they last in this territory . . .'

Bradley was silent for a while, as Skreech turned and turned his cane.

'What does Red Dog get out of it?'

'Out of what?' The edge had returned to his voice.

'Out of the arrangement with The Mount.'

'What the other warlords get. He gets to trade with the Invisible City. He gets this territory to call his own, as long as he patrols it and keeps unwanted people out of the Invisible City.'

'Like who?'

'Like you, me, homeless, parentless us.'

'You don't have to be here,' said Bradley, slowly and deliberately.

'Shut up, just shut up!' Skreech was on his feet, his stick rattling along the bars of the cage. Hunger leaped up, snarling, throwing himself against the bars, till Bradley pulled him down.

'It's all right, Hunger,' Bradley whispered to him. 'It's all right.'

Victor too was up, agitatedly going from one side of his cage to the other, his head rocking from side to side, till Bradley called out, 'Victor, Victor, it's OK, it's OK. Be still.'

The three of them lay back down, but Hunger and Victor continued to sift the air, their eyes alert. How long they stayed like that – minutes or hours – Bradley couldn't be sure. While he drifted off to sleep, they remained locked in a timeless immobility.

Bradley only wakened when there were heavy footsteps and the door was flung open.

The room soon filled with the boy soldiers. Then, with accompanying clapping, stamping and whooping, and bursting from a red pinafore dress, Red Dog entered, behind him the weasel.

Beside the weasel ambled the tawny mass of Red Dog's champion, its shoulder muscles rippling as it walked. It didn't stand quite as tall as Hunger, but, like a burst sofa, it made up for that in breadth. Its head was almost square, half of one of its ears had been ripped off in some previous encounter. A scar ran across one eye. This was a trained, experienced fighter, but Bradley noted that, even as it walked, it panted. If Hunger were fit . . . Yet Bradley couldn't know how much yesterday's struggles had taken out of him. Certainly, if that brute got its jaws fastened round Hunger's throat, the fight would be over.

'Good morning, my hearties. Oh, I always loved the pirates. They were the very best stories, don't you think? Oh, don't you, don't you? Answer me!'

This was spoken – shouted – at one child in particular – one with a pale face crossed by a flop of hair.

'Yes, Red Dog, the best.'

'Oh, good, good, but Red Dog . . . Red Dog's noticed you. He *knows* you now.'

The boy gulped and everyone else seemed to become even more buoyant.

'But-but-but,' Red Dog machine-gunned round the whole company, 'that might not be the way of it, because you know, you just know how much Red Dog loves numbers – how much he adores the number . . . eighteen. Oh, six times three – lovely! Oh, two times nine – glory! Now where do I begin?'

The boys began to shuffle.

'No one move,' screamed Red Dog and pointed to the flop-haired boy. 'Here, I'm going to begin here. A one and a two and a three and a four . . .'

Rooted to the spot, once ten had been passed, the next group of boys fidgeted and silently pleaded.

'. . . and a . . . sixteen . . . and a . . . seventeen . . . and a . . . ay . . . ay . . . eighteen!'

Number eighteen boy yelped.

'Fix him as a possible too, Laugh-tenant,' said Red Dog, visibly tiring of that game, before he remembered another.

'Now,' he said, turning to the cage, 'now to business. Oh, I love the early morning – the sunlight, the birds singing, joy in the heart.'

The closest boys all tried to put 'joy in the heart' expressions on.

'This now,' he said, pointing to the burst sofa, 'is Tender. Hunger – Tender. But I want you to meet him up real close. Key!'

The weasel handed him the key.

'Now you,' he said to Bradley, 'out.'

Bradley took Hunger's ears in his hands to look him eye to eye. 'Keep moving, keep away from the jaws. If not, you're done for.'

This is my fight now, said Hunger.

'Out now!' Red Dog bellowed. 'Now, let's shake things up a bit here.'

Bradley stood outside, children once more fastened to him, as the weasel rattled a stick up and down the bars. Bradley would have wanted Hunger to keep his strength, but Hunger's rage and hatred were so great, he threw himself, biting and snarling, against the bars.

'That's more like it, that's much more like it,' said Red Dog and pushed Tender hard up against the bars.

Tender realized that the only thing between the bars and him walking out of there to a celebratory meat bone was that black dog that seemed to hate him so much. Tender began to feel the same hatred, opening his huge jaws, angling his head to try to take a lump out of Hunger when he was up close.

'Good,' said Red Dog. 'Good. Very, very, very good. I think we're ready to rumble.' He signalled to the weasel, the door was opened and Tender, with his ambling gait, ran into the cage.

It was then that Hunger's appetite for the fight seemed to desert him. Whenever Tender came for him, he found space. Tender only had one move and he knew he could wait for it to bear blood. It was just a matter of time. Red Dog, ooh-ing and ah-ing, his nose almost to the bars, shared Tender's optimism.

Still, Tender's panting had become more noticeable, as he turned and turned again, tracking Hunger's flowing movement round the very rim of the cage. Every so often Tender hurled himself at the spot where his opponent should have been, only to ring against the bars. A couple of times his jaws clamped round Hunger's coat, leaving him with a mouthful of hair.

This encouraged him; surely, just a question of time.

Hunger appeared to be tiring. More and more frequently, Tender was launching these nearly-there attacks. Red Dog cheered. The boy soldiers cheered. To see his champion victorious again would make Red Dog happy; possibly make him overlook the few small things that could lead someone to The Mount – wipe the slate clean.

But they were all watching a different fight to the one Bradley saw. In his, a slow, old fighter was being suckered into close exchanges by a faster opponent. At first, up close, Hunger could get a sense of Tender's mass, a feel for his mobility. Later, a counter attack could be launched. And that was the way of it, when Tender lunged in one more time, his jaws closing – oh, so close – on Hunger's rump. Red Dog's face cracked open with anticipation. But before he could cheer, Hunger had birled round and snapped twice – two rapier bites – across Tender's head.

Only scalp wounds, yet blood poured down Tender's forehead, blinding him as, enraged and panting, he set off in pursuit again. But the noise of the crowd dulled his hearing, as the smell of his own blood veiled his sense of smell. His jaws hanging open, he felt as if he were chasing a ghost.

Now Hunger could attack relentlessly. Still careful to avoid the killer jaws – nothing now would be sweeter to Tender than to lock his jaws on Hunger's neck – he made darting runs at Tender, each time drawing blood – from a shoulder, from a back leg, from Tender's one good ear.

Tender stood now, drenched in blood, disheartened, in the centre of the cage, as Hunger, knowing that his work was done, circled him, emitting small, victorious growls.

'Ohhh,' groaned Red Dog, 'it's done, it's done. Someone pull that beast out.'

A pole was thrust against Hunger to hold him off, as the door was opened and Tender called out. Gratefully, Tender turned his back on Hunger and, trailing blood, left the cage.

'Take him away,' said Red Dog, sounding both disappointed and disgusted. Then he immediately brightened. 'Because, because, ladies and gentlemen, Red Dog, the only one – *once met, never forgotten; once crossed, better you were never begotten* – Red Dog has a new champion: Hunger, the black wolf!'

The children cheered, as they knew to do, and Bradley caught a glimpse of Skreech. A smile flickered on his lips, a real smile that vanished when Bradley mouthed at him, 'Hunger, my friend.'

Unable to see, but only to hear the cheering and the growling, the fight had been a draining experience for Victor. He sat in his rags, scratching himself.

'Victor,' Bradley shouted. 'Hunger won!'

'What's that to do with you, *Dog Boy*?' said Red Dog. 'Hunger's *my* champion now.'

And as night came on, Bradley could hear the boy soldiers chanting still – 'Hung-ger! Hung-ger! Hung-ger!' – even as tiredness flooded him and he sank into the deepest of sleeps.

CHAPTER 9

SOMETHING ROTTEN

Bradley is in the kitchen. It is one of the places he is not allowed, but he loves the way the light slants in from the high windows across the scarred wooden table and the way the dented copper pots hanging from the wall resemble a kitchen armoury. Besides, Margaret is here.

She is leaning into the deep white sink and holding a sieve of strawberries under a twist of water.

'Beats me why you're not supposed to be here,' she says. 'Vince and your father were never out of here as boys.'

'Really?' says Bradley.

'Lord, yes. And half the time I was the one back then wanting rid of them. "Look," I'd say, "I've got too much work to do to have you pair fighting around me all day." '

'Fighting?' says Bradley.

'Like dogs over a bone.' She gives the sieve a good shake and tips the strawberries into a white bowl. She brings it to the table. 'Here, have one of these, but for heaven's sake, watch your shirt and don't tell a soul. They're probably counted.' She smiles conspiratorially as they both bite into the sweetness.

'Why did they fight?' asks Bradley.

'Oh, you ask me! Brothers, that's why they fought. And different as chalk and cheese. Your father was the elder and his mother's favourite, no doubting that. Not that she didn't love your uncle Vince, but, well, your father was a born adventurer from the time he could walk. He was the first to climb the great oak, the first to build the bridge across the gorge – how he ever did that, I'll never fathom – and the first to glide from the castle walls. Like an albatross he looked, his bed-sheets pinned to the strawberry frames. At ten he went into business for the first time, marketing a range of soft drinks made from fruits from the estate. When people began to complain that they tasted vile and stained their lips and tongues, he remarketed them as dyes. *Salesman?*' Margaret smiles. 'I tell you, he could make you think Monday was Friday.'

'And Uncle Vince?'

'How could Vince compete? At every stage, your father had him beaten and Vince never had the imagination to discover things for himself. He seemed to be like a rabbit caught in headlights. He went one way, then another, but couldn't escape the glare of your father's successes – or even his wonderful failures. And the trouble was, neither could their mother. Charmed, she was. Absolutely charmed. I saw it coming, mind. I saw no good would come of it. Even when I'd say to her, "Look what Vince has made today, a papier-mâché volcano," she couldn't help remembering your father's volcano, brought for her birthday into the grand hall when the lights were out and erupting into all the colours of the rainbow. Aye, and filling the room with the smell of rotten eggs too! And I'm thinking now, that's the smell of jealousy – rotten eggs – and believe me, it's as foul a smell as you can imagine. Was it any wonder there were no tears of sympathy from his brother when your father lost his sight with that Vesuvius? Or tears at his funeral, you may have noticed—'

There is a stamping above them.

'Here,' says Margaret, 'that's the gamekeeper. He'd better not find you here.'

As they hear his steps coming down the stairs, Margaret ushers Bradley into the darkness of the deep pantry. She reaches up to one of the shelves stacked with glass jars and takes one, before closing the door.

'Ah, it's yourself,' says Margaret.

'And who else would you be expecting?' asks the gamekeeper.

'Don't be thinking my courting days are done,' says Margaret.

'Away, ye old crone,' says the gamekeeper, yet not unkindly. 'I'm your visitor for today.'

'Well, you'll stay for a scone and jam then. But get your hands away from these strawberries. They're counted.'

'I believe you.'

Bradley can make out through the slatted door the gamekeeper sitting side on to the table; one forearm resting on it. The gamekeeper brings the other arm up from the shadows and lays a long thick strip of fur on the table. The sun strikes it and turns it as coppery as the pans.

'There's another for the collection,' he says.

'Get that thing off my table,' says Margaret. 'There's food gets prepared on that, you fool.'

'Keep your hair on, Cleopatra. It's only a fox's brush.'

'I know fine what it is. I've eyes in my head. I just don't want it in my kitchen.'

'Aye, I know. And neither do I.'

The gamekeeper dips his head and a silence falls between them.

'You don't like killing the foxes, do you?' asks Margaret.

'Oh, if it has to be done, I'll do it. Never liked it, but if I saw a reason . . . Now, the old master and me, we saw eye to eye. We knew that most of the time, if you let it be, the natural world will find its balance; that some kind of harmony will establish itself. We never had peacocks strutting the lawns to defend, like now. All the chickens were safely cooped. So we never feared foxes. But now, now the new master's in, it's war.'

'War?'

'Aye, of a kind. You know, almost everything's gone now. The woods are near to silent, the tracks bare. There's one creature out there, though, that we haven't got the better of.'

'Only the one?'

'Aye, but he's special. A wolf. And it must be the last one there is, because they're social animals, wolves, and I've never seen him with another creature.'

'So you've seen him often?'

'Oh aye, lots. But he's that quick and clever, he's always one step ahead. I see his eyes in the darkness between branches, glittering like fireflies, or I catch the grey streak of him crossing a clearing. But when I get there, nothing. Tell you what though, that wolf and I have an understanding.'

'Don't tell the master that,' says Margaret.

'Do I look stupid?'

'No,' she says firmly, 'but nor do you look like

someone who's come here to court me, so time you were gone.'

'Aye, time we were all gone from here. There's something rotten gone on and I hate to be a part of it.'

Margaret stops and turns. 'What do you mean "something rotten"?'

'I mean that Vince has come into this property – aye and much more – in a very shady way.'

'Shush now. You shouldn't be talking this way.'

'No?'

'No, it's easier if we just—'

'Carry on? Tell me you don't have your suspicions.'

'I told you, I don't like to say.'

'Well, I've a lot more than "suspicions".'

'Oh, but keep your voice down.'

Bradley lays his ear against the slats, not to miss anything.

'What's to tell?' says Margaret.

'It all began,' says the gamekeeper, 'with a card game.'

Looking down at the dog boy, Skreech saw him frown, before he buried his head deeper in the blanket scraps he lay on. Hunger's silver chest touched him with every breath he took. It was a handsome dog, right enough. Even when he was writhing helplessly in the net, there had been something magnificent about him. Skreech had noticed how some of the boy soldiers, meeting his wild eyes, had retreated back into the group, their taunting sticks dragging on the ground. Now, the dog seemed to sleep peacefully, exhausted from the fight. Only his sharp ears gave an occasional involuntary twitch. The boy's sleep was more troubled.

But he wasn't the only one. Skreech heard from the great hall the sniffling, the broken cries, the unbidden shouts, as what was masked during the day, was revealed. All the homes still grieved for. The mothers still missed. And those who had managed to bury their needs deep within themselves lashed out at those whose surfaces were so easily read.

'Shut it, will ya!'

'Put a sock in it!'

'You want something to cry about, do you?'

Most of them learned to wear disguises; though there was no disguising the fear that seeped into the mattress at night. Fists laid into the culprit come morning.

'You dirty little beast.'

'How old are you? Two?'

'This'll sort you!'

And then there were the quiet revelations. The scratching of old sores. The forearm that never healed. The thigh that looked as if it had been combed with thorns. The nails, like that Victor's, bitten down to the quick.

The boy and the dog must be exhausted, Skreech thought, to sleep through all that. He remembered his first nights here – the hours lying staring at the cracked and peeling walls, surrounded by the restless sleepers. Yet it was not simply the sounds that had kept Skreech awake back then; it was the relief of feeling safe. No matter how unpleasant or how dirty his new 'home' was, he had felt a part of something for the first time in a long while and it had seemed to him then that being a part of something was the only way to survive.

'So much love in the world,' Red Dog would bellow. 'So much love. Yet who loves Red Dog? I ask you, who loves Red Dog?'

And the earnest faces would chant, 'We do! We do! We do!'

But it had not been long before Skreech realized they were all in competition with each other for Red Dog's favours – and it was Red Dog's mask they all had to learn to wear.

Talking to the dog boy, Skreech had felt his own mask begin to slip. It was unsettling, like a rush of air in a stagnant room. And he knew if he were not to lose all he had, he would have to be very careful.

'I was there,' the gamekeeper says.

'Where?' says Margaret.

'The card game, I'm telling you. I think I was there as

a stooge. To make it look as if it was a harmless game of cards. But it wasn't.'

'You're talking in riddles,' says Margaret.

'Give me time to unfold my story,' says the keeper. 'It's a hive in my head day and night and I must share it with someone.'

Bradley sees the gamekeeper grasp Margaret's fore-arms and bring her down in the seat before him.

'Right now, keeper, calm yourself. It can't take for ever to tell.'

'It'll take what it'll take,' the gamekeeper says, so strongly that Margaret lays her hand across the hand that grips her and strokes it gently.

'Aye, come on then. Tell.'

'It was the night of that last big storm. Do you remember it?'

'How could I not? It put the great oak across the driveway; it toppled the gable chimney.'

'Aye, I remember the barks of the foxes and the howls of the wolves – everything saying, We're here in this together against the fierceness of the wind and the rain.'

'Hot soup, I remember,' Margaret says, 'this request for a pot of hot soup. Vince would be staying over and the mistress would like hot soup for everyone, to burn out the dampness we all felt.'

'Yes, well, it was me who brought up the last two

bowls to the gaming room – one for Vince and one for the master. I laid them down and was just about to leave, when Vince said to the master, "Here, how about a game of cards to while away a nasty night? Keeper, will you join us?"

'Naturally, I turned to the mistress to see what she would make of this. I'd never spent time upstairs with them at all before.

' "What a splendid idea," she says to the master. "Don't you think so?"

'The master smiles that devilish smile of his and says, "Indeed, my love, I'm feeling lucky tonight. What about you, keeper?"

'Well, I draw myself up and say, "I don't rightly know, but I'm willing to give it a go, if you'll guide me in the cards."

'That's when Vince pipes up. "Oh, keeper, it's just a folly to fill an hour, while the storm blows itself out. Luck and skill aren't so important as your company."

'I have to say, I wondered even then what he could be wanting with my company, never having sought it before. But I couldn't think of a reason to refuse, so I sat as they finished their soup. Odd to watch the master dipping that spoon unerringly into the bowl and bringing it to his lips without once dipping his head or spilling a drop.

'The bowls were laid on a tray to the side. "Oh, I do

prefer informality," I remember the mistress laughing, as Vince asked for the cards. The mistress took them from a drawer by the window. Vince broke them open and began to shuffle.

'How can a blind man play cards? you're asking. Well, it's no mystery to me now. When the hand was dealt, I could feel the tiny patterned blisters of Braille on each one. So while Vince and I looked at our cards, the master, his blind eyes held at exactly the same level as when he'd taken his soup, rubbed the corner of each card gently with his thumb.

'The slightest smile never left his lips. That's what beat me the first time. I thought the smile betrayed a winning hand and I threw mine in – the best hand I got all night too! But soon I realized this was his card-playing face. The smile gave nothing away.'

'And what were you playing for?' asks Margaret.

'Nothing at first. That is, matches. Then, when matches lost their attraction, we played for candles. Each of us with a great box beside us and the mistress laughing, "Oh my, what boys you are!" She sat on the arm of the master's chair – she could see his cards clearly – and the same smile played around her lips too, but more so, as if she delighted in how the master's stack of candles rose.'

'So where's the—?'

'Give me time, woman, I'm coming to it now.'

Bradley takes a deep breath and lets it out very slowly, his eyes following along a line of preserves – Gooseberry, Apricot, Raspberry, Cherry – each one with a date he cannot read in the darkness.

' "Oh, brother, there's little sport in this," says Vince all of a sudden and he points to the rain lashing the window. 'We need stronger diversion than a game *for candles* to keep the likes of that at bay."

' "Perhaps you're right," replies the master, tapping his pile of candles. "Still, perhaps the storm bothers you more than it does me. I admit to liking the sound of the wind and the rain. They speak to more than the eyes, like a message to my unsighted world."

' "Mmm," says Vince – and if it was a message, then what happened next told me the master wasn't receiving it. For the master asks, "Well, Vince, what do you suggest?"

' "I suggest," says Vince, laughing as he says it, as if no one knew the sheer fantasy of it more than he did, "playing for the estate."

' "For the estate?" says the master. But you know, he never said it with any kind of incredulity at all. It was almost as if Vince had asked him to play for a picnic hamper.'

'Oh, that was him all right,' says Margaret.

'How do you mean?'

'That's the way he always was with Vince. Whenever

a challenge came, he wouldn't shirk it. But then, he never lost . . .'

The gamekeeper licks his lips. 'Just one of these strawberries. I need some juice in my mouth.'

'I'll get you a glass of water.'

'No, sit,' says the gamekeeper and he wipes a hand across his lips.

' "And what will you be wagering?" says the master.

' "Oh, this is too silly," says the mistress, but the master lays a hand on her arm and smiles.

' "Perhaps," he says.

' "Oh, of course it is," says Vince. "It's the storm has befuddled my brains with daft notions."

' "Answer me," says the master.

' "Well, I suppose, if I were to do this, I'd have to wager my portion of the estate – my two farms and the house I live in."

' "A fair house," replies the master.

' "Oh indeed," says Vince, "but nothing as grand as your inheritance." And though he said the words lightly, it was plain to me what he could not see, the face twisted with jealousy.'

'I knew it,' says Margaret.

'Wait,' says the gamekeeper. 'The master then turns his head towards me. "And what," he asks, "will you be wagering, keeper?"

' "Well, I don't reckon I've anything—"

'He doesn't let me finish. "Anything precious," he says. "For that is all Vince and I are wagering. That which is most precious to us."'

'Oh my lord,' says Margaret, 'can I bear it?'

'You must,' says the gamekeeper, 'for I have had to.

' "Well," I say, "I have my dogs and my cottage, but if I lose them, I'll have nowhere for my family and I'll never be able to afford such dogs again. You gentlemen will always have a roof over your heads. I beg to be excused this hand."

' "That's fair," says the master.

' "Perfectly," says Vince.

' "Just like two boys," says the mistress again.

' "Get a pen, my love," says the master, that smile, I swear, never leaving his lips. And Vince looking as though one of the lightning bolts we saw crossing the sky outside had electrified him.

' "Oh really!" says the mistress. But still she writes as they dictate to her their bills of deed and sign them.

' "Keeper," says the master, "perhaps you'd be good enough to cut the pack for us." Which I do. Then they each cut for who should deal. Vince draws an eight of spades, the master a jack of diamonds. Neither takes this first blood as a good or as a bad omen. The master still smiles; Vince's hands can't wait to get hold of the cards he is dealt.

'Two face up. Three down. Vince grabs at his first. I see his jaw clench, a line of sweat on his upper lip, but the master's expression doesn't change as he runs his thumb over the corners of his cards.

'Two aces lie face up before the master. Two queens before Vince. The master asks Vince if he would like any other cards, as if he was offering a second cup of tea. Vince asks for one and clutches for it before it hits the table.

' "Happy?" the master asks.

' "Happy," says Vince.

' "And I'll change these two," says the master. "And that's me too."

'So they're about to show their cards, when the mistress gets up, complaining about the draught. But instead of securing the window, she somehow or other manages to spring it open. The curtains billow into the room across the table and the master brings his hands down on his cards, but not before a couple have been brushed off the table.

' "Keeper, help me with the window," she says and, as I close it, looking hard for what the fault may have been, I'm aware of the mistress on the floor, picking up the master's cards.

' "What a business," she is saying, "and to come at such a time."

'She lays the cards before the master, who has stayed

still throughout, his hands spread over his remaining cards, which include the two aces.

' "Ready to show?" says Vince.

' "Madness," trills the mistress for the last time.

' "Ready," says the master.

' "I'll go first," says Vince and he turns over one more queen and a pair of jacks.

' "Oh," says the mistress. "Three queens and a pair of jacks."

' "Good, Vince," says the master, "but not quite good enough." And he pushes forward his two aces and turns over two tens and a nine. He turns them over slowly, as if the cards can speak for themselves, but the cards aren't saying what he wants them to say.

' "I think," says Vince, "you're mistaken, brother," and his voice is charged and coarse. "A pair – even aces – never beats three of a kind."

' "A pair? A pair?" The master grabs his cards and feverishly rubs and rubs at the corners of each, but nothing he finds there can add another ace to the two he has shown and our eyes have already told us he has lost.'

'My God,' says Margaret.

'Aye,' says the gamekeeper, 'that's what he said too: "My God."

' "Oh, my love," the mistress says. *Oh my love*,' says the gamekeeper in an ironic echo.

'How so?' asks Margaret.

'How so? Because there was something fishy in that game from the beginning. Something rotten and I smelled it and did nothing about it. But do you know what? I think the master thought so too – only he was too proud to get out of it; or more strangely, it added to the excitement somehow.'

'Aye, he never ever feared Vince.'

'His mistake was in thinking it was only Vince he was facing.'

'Dangerous talk, keeper,' says Margaret.

'Which is why I'm for leaving,' says the gamekeeper. 'It was only the master's inventiveness that kept this estate together. Without it, mark my words, it'll be in ruins in no time at all.'

'Aye, ashes and dust,' says Margaret, 'ashes and dust. And the estate meant everything to the master. Everything.'

'I know it too,' says the gamekeeper, 'but you know *all I heard* was that "My God".'

'Meaning?'

'Meaning, I don't know what. But after he said it, he tipped his head back and opened his mouth and, though no sound came out that I could hear, there came from the depth of the forest, through the wind and the rain, a howl so deep and so pained, it seemed to fill that room. The master then brought his head down and he rose from the table with that slight smile back on his face, no sign that his heart had been broken. He still had the business, of course, but that accident on the ice . . . Well, put it this way, those who say it was an accident don't know my story.'

There is a silence before Margaret says, 'Keeper, we'll talk further, but in the meantime—'

'I must go,' says the gamekeeper.

As he takes the steps up, Margaret opens the door of the larder. Bradley turns from the sudden light and notices, on a table at the back of the pantry, the tiered wedding cake, topped with the initials of his mother and his uncle Vince.

CHAPTER 10

THE HOUND OF HELL

Once sunlight filtered through the high, broken windows, it became a light of dust and ashes. But it was enough to wake Bradley. He sat up and pushed himself back against the bars of the cage. He rubbed the stiffness from a shoulder; lifted his trousers from the grazes on his knees.

Hunger raised and lowered an eyelid. His eyes were dull, as if their flames had been extinguished. Victor was still buried in his heap of blanket bits. Skreech, his head against the window and his mouth in a perfect O, slept on. His small hands cradled his stick.

Bradley rubbed his eyes. He had had such dreams before. Generally, he shook them from him, the way he did the Old Woman's stories. You had to come back into the world in which you were forced to live, and living needed all your concentration. And the stories, well, the Old Woman always said he carried them somewhere inside himself. Some seemed like warnings not to go back; others not to go forward. Fine, he would nod, that way they needn't interfere with his here and now.

But this morning it was different. He shook his head and, though he found the details of the story scattered like water shaken from a dog's back, the dream's shape seemed to fill him and all day he could not shift the sense of loss he felt.

Skreech's head tipped forward and he rubbed his neck and circled his head. He looked across at Bradley and at Victor. Both of them stared into the space before them; whether at the bars of their cages, at the walls beyond, or through them both, he could not tell.

Along with the light – thin though it was – time had entered the room. Bradley had never experienced it in such a raw form as he had in the last days. Like black syrup, it coursed through him, making him heavy, filling him with despair. When your whole life was concerned with survival, what did you do, when you didn't know what there was to be done?

He saw in Victor's eyes a despair that matched his own. And, as the day wore on, he noticed more and more that Skreech displayed the same listlessness, the same sighing emptiness he himself felt. Bradley showed nothing, but the recognition confirmed for him what he had suspected: that Skreech was their best chance of getting out of there.

As the grey light thickened with evening, a boy soldier brought Skreech a large bowl of clean water and a plate of meaty slops for Red Dog's champion – and a plate of thin porridge for Bradley and Victor. The weasel unlocked the door of the cages and Skreech placed them inside.

'Watch that dog – it's a killer,' said the weasel, but Bradley could see that Skreech wasn't scared of Hunger.

Once the weasel had left, Bradley called across, 'You like this dog, don't you?'

Skreech said nothing, but Bradley saw his bruised jaw-line harden. He would give nothing away.

'Makes no difference,' Skreech muttered from his corner, as Hunger licked out his food dish and slurped up the water.

'What?' said Bradley.

'He's going to die anyway.'

'Maybe not.'

'Red Dog's champions never last long. You saw that.'

'Yes, but Hunger's got a fighting chance.'

'For a while.'

'And you?'

'What about me?'

'For how long have you got a fighting chance?'

'Long enough.'

'Oh, come on, look at it. You said it yourself – who knows when Red Dog's going to see some tiny thing in you that displeases him? This week? Next week? Next month? Next year? It's going to happen.'

'I take my chances.'

'Yeah, but reckon your chances. There are – what? – forty of you – that makes it forty-to-one in my book. These are running-out odds.' The Old Woman had taught him that too.

'Yours any better?'

'Yeah, they are. Risky but not impossible. You join us and—'

'You nuts?'

'No, desperate.' Bradley thought he saw the flicker of a smile pass over Skreech's face too. It was time to let him start running the conversation.

Bradley stroked Hunger's head as he settled. Hunger sighed heavily twice, as if to rid himself of the day's boredom.

Bradley waited.

'Huh, what would I get out of it?' Skreech made it sound like a question that didn't deserve an answer.

'You get to take your chances with us.'

'Like, why on earth—?'

'Victor, Floris, Hunger and me, we're a . . .' Bradley had never thought what they were beyond some version of a dog pack. Yet how was he to explain what that meant – that it meant more than what bound all Red Dog's boy soldiers together?

'We look out for each other. And if you helped us, we'd look out for you.'

'Friendship – pah. I told you, I don't believe in any of that stuff.'

'Here, sure, I can see why you don't. But outside it's different, it can work.'

'This is stupid, talking about this. Stupid. Anyway, it's impossible.' But Bradley heard, in Skreech's dismissal, the hesitant desire for it not to be so.

'That door over there, back of the room, where does it lead to?'

'Nowhere.'

'Nowhere?'

'It used to lead into another block of apartments, but they were torched in the Dead Time and torn down. There's just the stairs now down to the street. It's how the cages were brought up. But the door's always locked.'

'Who's got the key?'

'The lieutenant keeps it. He likes keys.'

'Yeah, I've seen that.'

'Is the door used much?'

'No.'

'Then he wouldn't miss the key. Look – sometime,

could you make an excuse to get the whole bunch and to slip that one off – maybe when the cage needs to be opened?'

'Maybe.'

'That would be the first stage, then we need to see how things develop. The next fight will be here, right?'

'Yes, Red Dog always has home advantage.'

'Good. Look, we're all going to get out of here.' The boy sniffed. 'With your help,' Bradley added.

'Sure,' Skreech said. 'Sure.' But it did not sound as if he believed it for a moment.

The rest of that day, Skreech turned his back on Bradley's cage. He drew and rubbed and drew again on the dusty window. Whenever Bradley called to him, Skreech told him to 'Shut it, will ya.' Bradley felt his whole body go limp as he waited to be betrayed.

The next time the boy soldier came in with food – the usual slops and gruel – the weasel opened Bradley and Hunger's cage for him. But the boy only had scraps for Victor. He flung these through the bars. Victor was especially agitated.

'Oh, Lieutenant,' said Skreech, rousing himself, 'look at him. He just hates the sound of these keys. Watch!' He took the keys from the weasel and rattled them up and down Victor's cage. Victor went crazy, jumping at the bars, snarling and spitting.

The weasel bared his teeth with delight. 'Oh, perhaps there's a little bit more fun left in you after all.'

That's when Hunger and Bradley went wild. Bradley took up the tin bowl and hammered it against the bars, as Hunger whooped and howled.

'Hey, this is a circus. It's going to be some Christmas party tomorrow.'

When Bradley and Hunger had calmed down, the boy was standing before the weasel with his keys. The weasel took them and clipped them back onto his belt.

'I can't wait,' he chortled as he left.

Bradley and Skreech sat silently for a while, waiting for their breathing to even out. Hunger panted in bursts and Victor could be heard moving around his cage, muttering to himself.

Skreech came over and slipped the heavy skeleton key through the bars and Bradley hid it under the rags. If it were noticed missing, no one would think to look for it there.

Skreech sat back down, blinking, unnerved by what he'd done.

'That was a brave thing.'

'Shut it,' Skreech said. 'It's done.'

'What will happen tomorrow?'

'Sometime, you never know when, Black Fist will arrive with his soldiers and his champion. We'll all cram in here. Bets will be placed. The fight will begin.'

'That's all you know?'

'That's it.'

'Right, listen to me. You must – tonight – unlock that door and place the key on the outside. We'll hope no one needs to use it. The fight will be noisy. At its end, the cage will be opened to pull one of the dogs out. That will be the time of the greatest commotion, yes?'

'Yes.'

'OK, now whichever dog wins . . . whichever dog, there needs to be some distraction.' Bradley was thinking back to every ruse the Old Woman had ever used, but he couldn't as yet find something which he thought might work. He would not sleep that night until he did. 'In the distraction, Victor, Hunger and I will escape.'

Oh, let it be you, Hunger, thought Bradley, *let it be you.*

Hunger had his eyes fixed on Bradley: *While there is breath in me, I will fight.*

'Oh, so easy, eh?' Skreech said bitterly. 'Like, Victor's locked up – or haven't you noticed?'

'That's something I need to work on.'

'I should give up on this now.'

'Trust me. I never said it would be easy.'

'And after?'

'Tell us where to wait and we'll meet . . . Then we'll go to get Floris.'

'Crazy,' Skreech said. 'All of us crazy.'

Bradley noticed the 'us', but did not want to press it.

* * *

It was late afternoon the next day before Skreech placed a bowl of scraps for Hunger in the cage and the weasel waved Bradley out.

'Time's getting close,' he said. 'I hope for your sake that your dog's up for it.'

Bradley gave Hunger a stroke, a firm stroke all down his head. It was the one that forced his head back, that made their eyes meet.

'Whatever happens, I know you'll find a way to pull through.' Bradley said the words with clenched teeth.

While there is breath in me, I will fight.

'He'll be ready,' Bradley told the weasel. 'But he'd fight stronger and longer if he could hear me *and* Victor both shouting him on.'

'Get out of it,' said the weasel.

'Look, just think about it for a minute. Hunger sees himself as part of a pack. Yeah, silly, isn't it? All the same, he feels when he fights that he's fighting for the members of the pack.'

'And that's you and that . . . creature over there.'

'Exactly. What have you got to lose? I'm not saying it'll be decisive, but if this fight's going to be as hard as I think it is, we need every advantage we can get.' Bradley hated to use that 'we', but he too was prepared to use anything for an advantage. He could see the weasel's face narrow in thought.

'I mean,' Bradley pushed, 'think if Hunger lost and Red Dog knew that—'

'All right, shut it. You,' the weasel said to Skreech, 'come here. You're going to go into that cage, clip this lead onto the creature's collar and bring him over here. You, Dog Boy, tell that thing to behave.'

'Victor,' Bradley called over to him. 'Victor, don't fight the boy guard. Be calm.' Victor looked at Bradley with his wide, empty eyes and nodded slowly twice.

The weasel unlocked Victor's cage and Skreech clipped the lead onto his collar and handed the end of it to another soldier, a mean-looking boy with hollow cheeks and dark-rimmed eyes. As he brought him over, Victor tried to stand, but the boy pulled on his lead and Victor was brought down, choking, onto all fours.

'Good, that's the way,' laughed the weasel. The boy tugged the lead more for the weasel's amusement.

The weasel took the lead and tied it round the bars of the cage. 'There we are then, thing, there's your perfect viewing spot. Aha, I think I heard footsteps.' Then he turned swiftly to Bradley. 'You'd better be right about this, Dog Boy. If you're not, you'd better start praying.'

The door was flung open with the usual banging and whooping as Red Dog entered, a mass of crimson chiffon billowing behind him. An ungainly boy soldier, who somehow had become caught up in the doorway with him, was held, then kicked sprawling to the floor.

'So, so, so, once again, ladies and gentlemen, welcome Red Dog, the only one – *once met, never forgotten; once crossed*— What's this?' He broke off, pointing to Victor.

'Ah, tactics,' said the weasel importantly.

'Tactics?'

'Yes, tactics. I think that dog will fight harder if the creature's watching with Dog Boy. They're pack dogs, you see.'

'Clev-er, clev-er. You are the best of laugh-tenants,' said Red Dog. The weasel beamed.

'But to return to formalities . . .' Red Dog rose up to his full height, his periwig causing the lowest crystals of the chandelier to tinkle together. 'For a Christmas treat, Red Dog has invited, to share the joys of canine combat, his esteemed neighbour, the great warlord, Black Fist!'

Immediately, a guard of honour formed – six boy soldiers each side and all blowing furiously on small plastic trumpets. As Victor put his hands to his ears and rocked and whined, Hunger tore round his cage in fury.

At the end of the fanfare, two other children appeared, pulling a small trolley on which stood a mountain of a man, draped in black. The trolley stopped and the man-mountain swayed. The children looked up at him, alarmed, till he had composed himself. He stepped off and Red Dog took his hand. Bradley noticed what small, delicate-looking hands Black Fist had.

'Welcome, Black Fist. Let me introduce you to my champion. His name's Hunger and he's hungry for blood.' Red Dog's face opened with his pleased-with-myself look and his boy soldiers banged approval.

Black Fist peered in at Hunger. 'Huh, it'll be a short fight then. My champion is undefeated in eight fights. No dog has lived that's stood against him. And this black creature will be no different.' Now Black Fist's soldiers yelped their agreement.

'We'll see,' said Red Dog. 'What he gives away in weight, he makes up for in spirit. Anyway, enough talk. Bring in your champion.'

Black Fist clapped his hands and four black-clad boy soldiers brought in a huge grey dog. His back was level with his escorts' shoulders, his long jaws heavily muzzled. His shadow moved like a frieze along the walls.

'This, Red Dog, and make no mistake, is the Hound of Hell.'

'Well, Black Fist, originality was never your strong point,' Red Dog sneered.

The Hound of Hell's black eyes looked madly around the room. When he sensed Hunger's presence, he shook his head and, in spite of the muzzle, grumbled in his throat.

Hunger too was aware his enemy had entered the room. His hackles were up and he was freely growling at the grey monster.

'Good, good,' said Red Dog. 'Just keep that up for a while, till we get our betting done.'

The weasel now came between both men, as they dictated to him what they were prepared to wager: sacks of potatoes, material for banners, knives . . .

Meanwhile, Hunger and the Hound of Hell snarled at each other and pushed against the bars that divided them. The children's eyes gleamed.

Red Dog and Black Fist slapped hands in agreement, then both turned to the cage.

'And now,' Red Dog intoned, 'the main event, this Christmas Day. This is a dog fight to find the Champion of Champions, a fight to the finish.'

Bradley glanced at Skreech. He scratched behind his ear, the sign they'd agreed on. The door was unlocked and everything else taken care of, as far as it could be. Whether or not they would be leaving with Hunger, they would soon know.

'Then begin!' shouted Red Dog to a clamour of shouting and whooping. The Hound of Hell's muzzle was slipped off, the weasel unlocked the cage and the Hound bounded in.

But what on earth was Hunger playing at? Faced with his greatest challenge, he had dropped to his elbows in an invitation to play. *Chase me*, he was saying. Moreover, his tail was up, radiating confidence.

'Your dog's gone mad with fear,' said Black Fist.

The Hound of Hell couldn't understand it either. His head was cocked momentarily, as he considered this impudence. He'd been insulted. *Chase you?* he snarled. *I'll chase the life out of you. You don't deserve to be in the same cage with me.*

Hunger easily avoided the first lunge. And the second. The Hound's effectiveness had been dulled by his rage. But now his head was clearing. He took command of the centre of the cage, his eyes riveted on Hunger, who stood low, silently baring his teeth.

With one great leap, the Hound was on Hunger. It was clumsy, but his weight toppled Hunger for an instant. The Hound stood over him and reached with his open jaws for Hunger's spine. As they closed on it, Hunger twisted out of reach and tore into the Hound's chest. Both had now drawn blood. Flesh wounds, yes, but both acknowledged the other's power to wound. When they looked at each other now, there was wariness mixed with the hate. The preliminaries were over. Both knew now that mind games wouldn't win this fight – only speed of reflexes, strength and determination.

The crowd filled the pause in the action with their clamour.

'That dog won't be so lucky next time,' Black Fist commented.

'We'll see,' said Red Dog. But he scanned his eyes worriedly down his wager all the same.

Victor had set up his own quiet chant: 'Hung-ger, Hung-ger, Hung-ger, Hung-ger, Hung-ger.' It didn't vary in speed or intonation, as if he were willing each breath of it into Hunger.

They had been shadowing each other round the cage for so long now that you might have thought neither dog was prepared for another move; that neither was prepared to face the slashing threat of the other's teeth. That was not the way Bradley saw it.

The next time it's all up with you, said the Hound.

Come on, then, said Hunger. *What are you waiting for?*

The Hound leaped. But this time Hunger was ready.

He brought his back down flush with the floor, almost in a cower, as the Hound hit against the bars of the cage. Then, twisting from below, he brought up his jaws and clamped them round the Hound's throat.

There was a choked growl from the Hound and he shook himself furiously, but Hunger knew this was his winning move and he clung on.

The Hound lowered his head and raked Hunger, his claws cutting into Hunger's back and chest. But Hunger held on, his mouth filling with the Hound's blood.

The Hound was weakening; his mad eyes roamed the room as he stood in the centre of the cage, Hunger - hanging from his throat. His head steadily lowered.

When the Hound of Hell eventually went down onto

his haunches and a little later fell over, Hunger was still fastened to his throat. Both were lying on the blood-stained floorboards. The Hound's glazed eyes already looked at Hunger from another world. His breathing was now a few gurgling rasps. Hunger released him and stood over him, his silver chest a bloody shield. He tipped his head back and howled weakly, as Red Dog's boy soldiers cheered.

'Well, Black Fist, I think that's the game over,' declared Red Dog. 'Go see to my champion, Dog Boy' – and he waved the weasel to open the cage.

That's when Skreech went into action.

He had wormed his way as close to Black Fist as possible, so that his black majesty could not help but notice, when Skreech seemed to spot something lying on the floor before him. Skreech's arms went out in surprise. *Cooler*, thought Bradley. *Cooler*. Skreech bent down to pick up the rag, from where he had only recently dropped it.

'What's this?' he said loudly, giving it a big sniff. 'Oh, wow, what is *that*?'

Black Fist grabbed the cloth from him and thrust his nose into it. It was only paraffin, but its fumes were enough to convince Black Fist his dog had been drugged in some way – or at least to persuade him that here was some excuse for not handing over his wager.

'Trickery!' he yelled. 'Your dog could never have

beaten mine without it. And here's the evidence. You dirty—' He lunged now in the direction of Red Dog, his great weight scattering the dense rows of boy soldiers.

'You loser, you!' Red Dog bellowed above the noise. 'Dirty cheat!'

Both sides of boy soldiers now launched attacks on the other, slapping, punching, spitting, wrestling each other to the ground.

In the commotion, Bradley unclipped Victor and called to Hunger. Skreech shouted to his boy soldiers to charge and so led them away from the corner of the room that led to the door.

Bradley, Victor and Hunger slipped through the unlocked door. Brightness slammed into them and, for a moment, their senses were frozen, before the lights of the Invisible City fell back and a dark chasm opened up before them. Bradley turned the key in the lock. A broken stairwell hung in the open space. They took the unsure steps as nimbly as they dared. They were at ground-floor level before they heard the banging echo above them.

On the street, they didn't look back. They knew it would not be long before the boy soldiers were out and swarming after them. Hunger carried a limp and Victor loped, his fists brushing the snow.

The alleyway, two streets away, was deep with slush, but it wouldn't take their footprints as clearly as the snow. At its end they crossed a street and came to a road running parallel with a river. There were steps down to its edge. They ran as close to the edge as they could; often the freezing water lapped over Bradley's and Victor's shoes.

At the third bridge they came to, they stopped. And they waited. Their breath, spilling out in clouds, seemed a huge giveaway. But it wasn't long before they saw the slight figure running along the river's edge. There were no others in sight, though the occasional cry of disappointment punctured the night and the faint roaring of Red Dog made them shiver more than the cold.

Skreech came in under the bridge and crouched, panting, beside them. No one said anything for a while. Hunger and Victor continued to sniff each other, bringing their stories up to date.

'Hunger all right?' Skreech said, eventually.

'Hard to tell in this light,' Bradley said. 'Once you think it's OK, I'll bathe his wounds.'

'Give it another hour,' Skreech said. 'I think we're in the clear. Most of them went the other way. No one would think you'd head for the Invisible City.'

'That was scary,' said Bradley.

'Yeah,' and Skreech let out a long exhalation.

'Some riot though.'

'Yeah,' he said. 'And Red Dog's face . . .'

'. . . will be something,' Bradley finished and they both smiled.

'Yeah, but he'll make someone pay,' Skreech said.

'But it won't be you.'

'No, not any more.'

'My name's Bradley . . . Bradley,' he said it again to fill the silence.

'Oh,' said Skreech. 'Yes.' Then he turned his face full on Bradley's. It was gloomy in there under the bridge, so although Bradley could see his eyes, he couldn't make out the expression he had on his face, when he told Bradley, 'Hi, my name's Martha.'

It took a dog's eyes to make out Bradley's astonishment. He caught the glint of Hunger's eyes on him.

I could have told you, Hunger said.

PART THREE

THE INVISIBLE CITY

CHAPTER 11

MARTHA

When Bradley woke there was a silver skin of mist floating above the river. Martha was crouched at the edge of it, cupping water and sluicing it over her face. Between times, she stayed perfectly still, moving her head slightly to the left, then to the right, as she listened to the morning. She turned, saw Bradley's eyes on her and turned back to the river.

She soaked the red rag she had worn round her arm, wrung it and brought it over to Hunger. She began to stroke his wounds gently to wash the remains of the Hound of Hell's blood from his chest.

'It's OK, boy, it's OK.'

Hunger raised his head to acknowledge her, then let it fall again onto the embankment.

'You like that dog,' Bradley said to her.

'Yeah, reminds me . . .' She turned away. 'He's a good fighter, that's all.'

Bradley let that stand, as he had let stand her admission the night before: 'We do what we have to do to get by.' Her eyes had flashed at Victor and at him then, as if to say, I am what I always was. Yet now, when Victor woke, clawing at his collar, there was no longer the hard edge of the boy guard Skreech in her voice, as she said, 'Here, I'll get that off for you.'

Victor looked at her, suspicious of the change and not yet ready to trust it.

'Come on,' said Martha. 'Why would I hurt you?'

Victor lowered his head and Martha unbuckled the collar. She gave a sympathetic tut at the deep scores round Victor's neck.

'Wait there.' She took the rag to the water's edge again and rinsed it of Hunger's dried blood, squeezed it and brought it back to Victor. Cold as it was, Victor rolled his head at the relief of it.

'Better?' Martha said.

'Mmm,' Victor answered.

They stayed there in the grey light for a while in silence: Bradley, Victor, Hunger and Martha. There seemed nothing more that needed to be said. They were out of one danger and about to enter another. Bradley knew they needed to gather their energies from some-where – to re-form the shared space, warmth and intention of the Pack. Yet how could he lead them when he didn't know the direction they must take? He felt the question like a fur ball in his throat, but he could not spit it out. Martha saw his proud eyes dart to her and away.

'Well, you can't stay here,' she said. 'Red Dog and the boy soldiers will be after you soon. Black Fist too likes a hunt. You need to cross over into—'

'What do you mean, *you*? Are you not coming with us?' said Bradley.

'I never said I'd come with you.'

'But you did. Back there, you did.'

'Look, you're out now. You can take care of yourselves from now on. I need to do the same. I'm going back to—'

'Back to Red Dog? But why?'

'Because it's better that way. I was very careful, no one will suspect—'

'But they'll find out. There's only you and two or three of the other guards who could've helped us to escape and by the time you get back, they'll all have told their stories. It would be madness to go back.'

'And madness to go on.'

'Yes, and remember it was madness to help us, but you did and we're out and you're with us.'

Martha dipped her head and covered her face with her arms. She began to rock slightly. When Bradley pulled an arm away, it was a very different Martha he saw. Gone was all Skreech's confidence, the way he used to slightly raise his head when he spoke, the way his experience came out as mockery, the way his jaw-line could tense into the hardness of a mask.

'I can't go back,' she said. 'I can't.'

'That's what I'm saying,' said Bradley.

'No, not to Red Dog. To the Invisible City.'

'You've *been*?' said Bradley. 'Been to the Invisible City . . .?'

Bradley noticed Victor becoming agitated, rocking on his heels and gently moaning.

'Yes, but I can't—'

'Yes, well, we must,' said Bradley. 'We must get Floris.'

We must get Floris, said Hunger.

'Floris,' said Victor, who had been moving closer and closer to Martha. 'Floris,' he whispered. 'Floris.'

'I can't – I . . .' Martha began.

Hunger had not followed the argument, but he had sensed the dramatic change in Martha's temperament; how the spirit of Skreech had drained from her. In the early days, when Bradley too was ambushed by some troubling vision from his past, Hunger had behaved no differently. He placed one front paw then the other on Martha's shoulders. Martha had to uncurl herself and lean forward to take Hunger's weight or else be pushed down onto the cold stone. Hunger stared at her and she saw herself reflected in those flame-yellow eyes. Her face calmed and she swallowed.

'We should be all right in the early morning,' she began, 'but we need to move fast. You must keep close behind me and not stop for anything.'

'Where are we going?' said Bradley.

'We'll head for a park I know. The Mount is not far from there.'

'OK.' Bradley turned to Victor and Hunger. 'You need to keep close, you understand?' He tapped the back of his thigh and Victor nodded.

'We're going to get Floris,' said Bradley.

'Floris,' said Victor.

'Let's go,' said Martha.

From the crumbling neighbourhood that had been their Zone, they had seen the light grow from the towers of the Invisible City, as they were rebuilt to the way they were before the Dead Time and the riots that had left them smashed and looted. Now, as the mist unwrapped them, their surfaces gleamed in the thin winter sunlight. Each glinting pane of glass, each strut of shining metal said, 'Keep out!'

They moved through shadows as far as they could. A few people clutching briefcases passed them in the opposite direction; all in a rush for one of the underground trains. The women's hair shone where it fell on their heavy woollen coats; it framed their grimly determined faces. They passed a glass-fronted coffee shop, where one of a row of men in creased suits looked up from his paper, half-stood on his stool as, wide-eyed, he said to his neighbour, 'Did you see what I just saw?'

At least that was how Bradley imagined it. For he and the others were long gone, down another broad road and another set of risks. But it was hard not to slow down passing the shops, which were just opening up for trade; hard not to stare a moment too long at the pyramids of apples, oranges, melons, the buckets of trumpet-headed flowers, especially for Christmas.

'Come on. Got to keep moving,' Martha pleaded – only she knew the full penalty of capture.

A woman carrying a heavy square attaché case and wearing matching gloves and shoes spotted Hunger and flattened herself against the side of a building that ended in the clouds. 'Oh my God, look, look! What is *that*?'

Hunger growled, low in his throat, in response. 'Come on, Hunger,' said Bradley and tapped his thigh again. But it was Victor, cage-cramped and terrified of the light surrounding him, who was having most difficulty keeping up the pace Martha was setting. And it was Martha, glancing round to check they were all together, who caught sight of the policeman coming out of another street. He was only five yards behind Victor and Victor had fallen five yards behind Bradley.

'Just stop there!'

Seized with panic, Victor did. And curled himself into a tortoise on the pavement. Bradley saw the smile on the policeman's face as he reached down for the scruff of Victor's neck – one down and the others wouldn't get far in the Invisible City. Not once he put the word out. The dog, huh, shot on sight.

The policeman was straightening up, pulling Victor up with him, when he caught sight of a streak of black in mid-air coming towards him.

Hunger knocked him backwards onto the pavement and latched onto the hand, which had reached too late for the stun-stick. The policeman yelled and tried to roll from Hunger's grip.

'Victor, Victor, come on,' Martha begged and Victor scrambled up and joined them.

'Now, Hunger, let go!' Bradley called.

They left the policeman nursing his bleeding hand, cursing. Let that black beast be someone else's problem, he thought.

'Almost there,' Martha called behind her.

The park was deserted, but Martha didn't let up. They ran under its green entrance and along paths, skirting grass, flowerbeds and a small pond, till the park began to thicken with trees. There was a small wooden hut in the trees, its slats green-edged and rotting.

'In here,' said Martha, tugging at the door. There were some old garden tools with broken shafts that Bradley spotted before Martha pulled the door shut behind them and they squatted, panting, in the darkness.

Bradley was aware of Martha's hand stroking Hunger's coat.

'You OK?' she asked Victor. Victor's eyes gleamed back at her in the gloom.

Splinters of day came through the cracked old wood. Eyes began to accustom themselves to the earthy light.

'Are we safe here?' asked Bradley.

'Safe nowhere,' said Martha, 'but few people use the parks now and this old hut—'

'How do you know this hut?'

'Doesn't matter.'

'No, but if you'd like—'

'Why would I?'

'You've risked a lot for us, Martha, I'd just like to know a bit more—'

'Nothing to tell,' said Martha, snapping off Bradley's interest as Skreech had once done. But there was, and when they had sat in silence a long time, her eyes staring straight ahead, Martha told it.

In the Dead Time, life in the Invisible City was little

different – the way Martha described it – to life in the Zones. People had to barter, beg and cheat to survive. Martha had had a dog then, Pepper, a black Labrador, and she wouldn't give him up.

A thought flared in Bradley's head: A bitch as black as coal, almost as big as himself . . .

Pepper had been a birthday present. Martha remembered the blunt black snout poking over the rim of the cardboard box, then the pink bow. How her parents' faces had glowed that morning – almost as brightly as her own.

'I'll find the food for Pepper,' she told her parents and she saved scraps from her own plate to feed her dog, whose haunches she still saw daily becoming more hollow. But then whose body wasn't going through a similar re-definition? Martha herself felt her ribs more clearly each morning.

As often as she could, she took Pepper to the park. The world of the park was a world they made themselves. Mostly, Pepper was still fierce enough to keep the odd drunk, who slept out on the benches, at bay; but when the gangs of boys began to roam the park, Martha would take Pepper to the old hut to sit out her fear in the darkness. Only one astonished old drunk had opened the door to find himself face to face with the black, snarling beast. He had never come back.

It could have been the gangs that got Pepper in the

end or it could have been one of the patrols that, after the Dead Time, began the ruthless clean-up of the Invisible City. It had to be done, everyone agreed, but in the enthusiasm to return to normality, to put the Dead Time behind them, there was little debate about what was implemented.

First, all stray dogs and cats were removed from the streets – they harboured, after all, who knew how many diseases. Then the case was made that all animals were suspect. Had they not mixed with the strays? Who could guarantee their pet had been kept inviolable? No one would get the opportunity to answer that question. The vans patrolled the streets; money was paid to street gangs for each animal they could deliver to the Animal Care Centres.

It was stray children – the street gangs themselves – who were next. The Dead Time had created many of these. It was a time of great change and there are always casualties in times of change. Sometimes it was the child's own decision: he was a mouth the family could not feed and he took himself off to try his luck in the streets. Sometimes, through neglect, it was the parents' decision that drove the child out. Or a mother, in exhaustion, would shake her head, stare at her child, as if her heart had turned to stone: 'What's to be done? What's to be done? What's to be done?'

Martha was lucky. Her parents had not weakened. In

fact, when Pepper disappeared, they saw it, not as Martha did, but as a sign of hope. Now Martha, pale Martha, would give herself every chance she could. They looked forward to seeing her chest fill out, the flutes of her ribs covered again with healthy young flesh.

But the other children, the ones who roamed the streets, living as they had during the Dead Time – thieving, begging, tricking – this was no way to carry on in a city that needed investors to have faith in it, that wanted to show the world that it had turned a corner and put the bad times behind it.

The vans that had collected the pets and the stray animals were renamed – Child Care – and the round-up of the children began.

The inhabitants of the Invisible City noticed the benefits immediately. They could walk down streets without being harassed; they need not carry their valuables in secret pouches, making their waists red and sweaty in the summer heat; they could use the smart leather attaché cases which were soon on the market with their various fur trimmings.

In the evenings now, people came out of their houses and strolled down the avenues. There was always something to see – a building restored, a new coffee shop opened, music playing out into the street, trays of nutty biscuits, foaming drinks and boards chalked up with exotic menus that changed daily.

Martha didn't see many other children now when she walked out with her parents, but the grown-up world seemed calm. 'Good morning.' 'Good afternoon.' 'Good evening.' Even the old greetings were coming back.

And, after all, those stray children were being so well taken care of. There were children's homes around the city – Wonderland, The Priory, Graceland – and each of them had won special commendation for the care shown to its 'clients'.

Still, there was no cause for complacency in the Invisible City. The particular knot of political and economic circumstances that had created the trauma of the Dead Time could not have been predicted, it was true, but steps could have been taken, which frankly had not, to protect the citizens – at least those of the Invisible City. Then, perhaps, let these lessons spread out to the other territories. But first make the Invisible City secure.

The answer the authorities came up with – an old-fashioned one certainly, but none the worse for that – was work. *Work. Work. Work.* Work, for, although the Dead Time is behind you, don't you still feel its stale, desperate breath on the back of your neck? And if you didn't, well, perhaps you were a shirker, a vagrant, a waste of resources. Then you might find yourself part of the cargo on a lorry heading back to the Compounds. It would slow down passing through the Zones and you would be thrown off like a sack of flour. 'Sure, you'll be welcome back, buddy. Just got to pass through the Forbidden Territories, that's all.'

Holidays were soon shortened as the working day lengthened. Someday the Invisible City would be able to afford to let mothers stay longer with their young children, to allow people to care for old relatives, but not yet. Now, everyone had their part to play: the builders to build, higher, faster; the teachers to teach, more and for longer; the cafés and quick-food outlets to provide more food and faster for working people who had no time to cook at home. Home, a place they visited only to sleep, to fall in front of a screen, which would be interrupted with visions of a wonderful world of leisure that lay somewhere far in the future. There were no evening walks now to choose an ice cream, to stroll round the park.

To begin with, Martha's parents were better off than most. Her father worked at the City University, a lecturer in Modern History, who had taken on the Dead Time as an area of research.

'We must learn from our past, Martha, if we are not to repeat our mistakes.'

Martha knew the serious face required of her at such times and she had nodded her agreement.

Many of his colleagues preferred to adopt a

philosophical approach to Martha's father's enquiries: *The Dead Time – beginning or end? The Dead Time, as a state of being*. Both had been the titles of papers delivered at conferences her father had organized. But Martha's father was most concerned with the *causes* of the Dead Time. Its effects he had seen with his own eyes: the suicides from the tall buildings, the individual personal tragedies that soon became shared, as the markets collapsed and the riots began. Fear and need had been everyone's daily companions then, till power gradually accrued within the artificial walls of the Invisible City and fear and need were banished to the Forbidden Territories and the Zones.

But the world had fragmented with the Dead Time. When one talked about it now, it was to one's own shrunken world that one referred. 'Putting one's own house in order' became the popular expression of these new divisions. Naturally, interests had had to shift – a point the principal had made to Martha's father at their last meeting.

'You have been a good *servant* of this institution,' he began. Martha's father had winced at the word, as the sharp-nosed principal peered at him through his round glasses. 'But you above all should be a student of how times have changed. We are living through a very unusual period, in which universities must prove themselves to be powerhouses for economic change. History, well, it's a luxury, isn't it?' Here he fingered the piece of Dead Time rubble on his desk. These popular mementoes were found in many offices and private houses, though not of course with such a fine brass mounting. 'A fascinating luxury, I grant you, but one that can best be pursued at leisure.'

For a while, the dismissal intensified Martha's father's obsession. There had been huge difficulties tracing relevant documents – so many had disappeared with the collapse of electronic communication – but he had begun to piece together a story concerning the causes of the Dead Time. When Martha took his explanations blankly, he said to her, 'The Emperor had no clothes. That is the root of the problem: all of us were spun a story – we invested, in a story, our wages and our dreams – but the Emperor had no clothes.'

Martha had felt it best to agree. 'I see, Dad,' she had said. 'Yes, I see it now.'

Martha's parents were now no different from many others in finding the demands of a working life and the raising of a family – Martha – incompatible. Each evening they returned to their flat long after dark, exhausted by work in their new clerical jobs and by the compulsory professional advancement. They had heard of the fine reputation enjoyed by some of the Homes – the caring teachers, the matron, the hearty meals and the after-school activities. Many, in fact, were open as day-care facilities. But becoming more popular was the working week facility. Parents were able to leave their child from a Monday morning till a Friday evening; thus they could concentrate with a trouble-free mind on work and on the evening classes which accompanied it, while their child could work at school and at homework and such, so that the weekend would be restored as a family-centred occasion. 'What are you going to do with *your* Family Weekend?' the slogan asked.

Martha and her parents spent the weekend avoiding each other's unhappiness. Her parents seemed so worn; all they wanted to do was sleep late, stare at the various screens, shop in the covered malls. Her father's research sat in boxes and gathered dust. Martha sensed their reluctance, their weariness, to face the questions she longed to ask: 'For how long?' 'Is there no other way?' 'Do you care for me at all?'

Certainly, her parents did not want to know about the bullying, short-tempered teachers, the vindictive games, the poor food, or the boredom. The Priory, after all, had been one of the best of all the homes; they had had it on good authority.

The first weekend they hadn't come to collect her, Martha had cried for the whole two days and they'd let her, lying there in the empty dormitory without a word of comfort. The next weekend there were apologies from her mother, tears. 'Oh, you don't know how hard it is, you've no idea.' Then, when Martha had pressed her for some kind of assurance that it wouldn't happen again, her mother's face with its red-rimmed eyes had twisted into an agony Martha could not bear to meet.

'What do you expect me to do?' Her mother whispered the words, as if in desperate prayer. 'What do you expect me to do?'

At the edge of the words, Martha smelled the spirit on her breath.

Whatever assurances Martha was given, they were not kept. Without reason or pattern, weekends were missed until one missed weekend was followed by another and another and another, till Martha lost count and realized she had joined the list of abandoned children. She felt attitudes to her had hardened long before matron told her one morning, 'Pack your bag. You're on the move today.'

'Where am I going?' Martha asked. 'Home?'

'Huh,' the matron replied. 'You'll see.'

One of the white vans took her the short journey from The Priory to The Mount – a short journey, but The Mount was a world away from the comforts of The Priory. For here were children, abandoned, stray, orphaned, who had no one who might care for them or even track their existence, which is more or less all Martha's parents had been doing till they had stopped caring and Martha had died to them. These were her gloomiest thoughts. Her best, though not exactly warming, were that her parents had decided she was better off without them. Whatever, Martha found it easier not to think about them - or at least to try not to. It was then she began to create the shell around her that had protected her until Hunger had reminded her of a time when she had felt love.

No one was interested in the children's education in The Mount – or only so far as it was useful. The Mount was one of a network of homes throughout the Invisible City where the electronics industry, upon which the city's economy depended, could be brought back to life. It was, at first, children's small, dextrous hands that were so valuable here – they could piece together the tiny components of all the electronic gizmos and screens that were needed once more. An ever-healthier market, and one that showed in all the graphs no sign of slowing, was personalized security. It was said that once you had installed your security system – no matter how expensive – it was already out of date.

The children sat at tables passing the machines up; each had a small repetitive job to do. Each machine was inspected on completion and if it were found to be faulty, there was some punishment imposed on the table responsible – a missed meal, a break taken away.

Two older children were assigned to supervise each table. Martha recognized a few of the boys from the gangs which had roamed the park. If a table was penalized, so were they and that was the worst of the punishment.

At night, they would come into the dormitory; the two alone or with other older children. Humiliation was always part of the punishment: name-calling – 'Pig-face', 'Thickhead', 'Sap'. And then the physical stuff – the head-slapping, the forcing you onto your knees and riding you round the room; the challenge for one inmate to fight the other. 'And do it proper or you'll be fighting me as well.' The supervisor children would look at each other then and laugh.

But that was for small offences. If you made any objection to the way you were treated, the quality of the slops you were served – worst of all, if you suggested, laughably, that you would appeal to a higher authority – you would be taken, stripped to your underwear and thrown into a freezing cold room for two or three days. It had not happened to Martha, but she had seen children come out of there pale and shivering, tracks of tears frozen to their cheeks.

'Floris.' Victor's voice filled out the darkness. Bradley too was remembering Floris: she was already pale and had a deep-seated cough. She would not survive such brutal treatment.

'It's OK,' said Martha. 'Floris will be too scared to challenge anyone yet. If she's kept her mouth shut and her fingers nimble, she should be all right.'

'How did you get away?' asked Bradley.

'I was lucky,' said Martha. 'They have pick-ups for the machines and for the rubbish. I knew if I was going to get out, it had to be with one of these. I was on a rubbish detail from the kitchen. I tipped the muck into one of the huge bins. Then I heard the lorry coming to collect it. I dived in and wormed my way under – not pleasant, but I wasn't caring about that. Then I felt myself ratcheted up and I was away. Someone had slipped up in his guard duty. When they tipped the bin out, they got a shock to see me rise from the muck. I slipped out their hands easily – I don't suppose they were too keen to grapple with me – and headed off as quickly as I could to the Forbidden Territories.'

'What if you'd been caught?' Bradley asked.

'Same as would happen now,' Martha said. 'I'd be damaged goods as far as The Mount was concerned. They'd have to make an example of me. It would be the cold room or worse . . . I'm not going back. Not ever.'

'Red Dog . . .'

'. . . is a brute. You saw that, but as long as I could make myself into a particular kind of person—'

'A boy soldier.'

'Yeah, whatever, then I could survive.'

Survival, thought Bradley, that was what their lives were about. It was survival that was stopping him reaching out to Martha, just as it was a threat to her own survival that she had broken a corner from her shell and was kneeling, stroking Hunger, sharing her story for the first time. It was Victor who sidled close to her, sensing that it was Martha rather than Bradley who could save Floris.

'What will we do?' said Bradley.

'In the early morning, when all these cracks are still filled with darkness,' said Martha, 'we'll go. Victor and Hunger must stay here.' Victor sat up, alert and quizzical. 'No. You both need to rest and to heal. It's too risky. Now lie low. Bradley and I need to sleep.'

CHAPTER 12

THE MOUNT

In the darkness, Martha tapped Bradley on the shoulder and they pushed the door of the hut open and stepped into the park again. It was a clear, cold night, a few clouds scudding over a full moon.

'This way,' said Martha and set off with her easy stride along the paths, out into the street. They moved through the Invisible City, always accompanied by their reflections in the glass building fronts, till they had cleared the main thoroughfares of the centre.

Martha pointed and there it was ahead, sitting on a slight hill: The Mount, its dark brooding shape squat against the inky sky. A few lights shone from its windows – for the rest, it was blind to the night.

They moved closer to the buildings and when they were in sight of the floodlit gatepost and entrance,

Martha veered off along the road which circled The Mount and soon both of them were pressed against the stone wall which surrounded it.

'This one's easy,' said Martha. 'Your top,' she commanded. Bradley handed over his hooded top and she took off her own and threw both over the glass-chipped wall top.

'You first,' she said and put her hands in a stirrup. 'Once you're over the wall, pull me up. And quickly.'

Bradley stepped into Martha's hands. She buckled the first time, but then shakily straightened, and Bradley heaved himself up. Astride the wall, they locked hands round each other's wrists and Bradley pulled her steadily up. Both of them fell off the wall onto the other side together. They lay close against the ground. Bradley felt her hard breathing against his ear and turned when she did to see the whites of her eyes, that wild glare of aliveness he had seen in Victor's eyes. They inched apart on their elbows.

The road wound its way up the hill to the main entrance; bluish lights at the edges marked the way.

'Now?' Bradley said.

'We need to cross the road, climb that bank on the other side. We're heading to that part that almost overhangs the road. OK?'

'OK.'

'Keep low, don't stop. Now.'

They got onto their haunches, then to their feet and climbed up the embankment. They glanced up and down the road before they crossed it. Bradley caught Martha in the full blue light, her face as it turned momentarily to him, her body low and perfectly balanced. At the edge of the road they leaped onto the opposite bank then scrambled through the dead leaves, watching for cracking branches, before they came to the overhang. Lying side by side, they looked out.

'We need to find out roughly the time the rubbish lorry comes,' said Martha. 'Can you tell time?'

'Roughly. From the sun. The Old Woman taught me.'

'Who?'

'The Old Woman. She's got a name too, but we knew her as the Old Woman—'

'Tell me sometime.'

'Sure. I will.'

They lay side by side, shivering on the cold ground, as the sun came up. Mention of her had brought the Old Woman back to Bradley. He thought of all her stories. Of how Thomas was forbidden to take food, of how there was a world the fairies took you to, from which you could never get release. He had thought that kingdom was Red Dog's. Now it appeared that it was The Mount. Even in sunlight, it was dark red sandstone, with the feeling of a prison. Yet there was a story with a different ending – one the Old Woman had hinted at, but never told. In it, the fairy kingdom would be equally daunting; but armed with wit, courage and luck, you might escape. Had they not already proved that it could be so?

When the sun was high and Martha and Bradley had been lost to their thoughts for hours, they heard the splutter of an engine. The lorry came up the hill, six black bins in its trailer.

'Empties,' said Martha.

It stopped as the front gates were opened, then it chugged through. The gates shut behind it.

'Now,' said Martha, 'start thinking time. When the lorry arrived and how long before it leaves.'

Slowly, Bradley plucked dead grasses. He had a pile of grasses and a bald piece of earth the size of a pillow when the gates finally opened again and the lorry drove out.

'Good,' said Martha, 'that should be long enough. Now we must wait for nightfall before we return to the park. Keep your eyes open for anything to eat when we do. There'll be lots of festive leftovers.'

Bradley pulled the door open and peered in. The hut was empty. He felt a chill seize him. Victor and Hunger had been taken; he and Martha were about to be captured. Bradley felt Martha's fear too before they both glanced about to assure themselves that whatever had befallen

Victor and Hunger, the danger had passed them by.

Bradley raised his head and gave two high-pitched howls. Martha seized his arm as they waited in the silence.

Then, a crack of twigs, the sound of rustling in the undergrowth, and Bradley could make out two shapes coming up the banking – one low to the ground, the other hunched and loping.

Hunger ran to Bradley, his eyes piercing, his teeth gleaming in the moonlight. Bradley stroked him and Martha went down on her knees to hug him. The black bush of his tail slapped against the open door of the hut.

'Victor,' Bradley said, 'what happened?'

'Men – loud, loud like Red Dog. Frightened us. We hid in bushes.'

'It's OK, Victor. It's OK.' But Bradley wondered how long Victor's nerves were going to last.

'Tomorrow, Victor,' Bradley told him, 'we will have Floris.'

'Floris,' said Victor. 'Floris.'

In the reclaimed darkness of the hut, between bites of old turkey pizza, Bradley outlined the plan Martha had formed as they lay side by side, the cold earth seeping through their clothing. It involved, simply, one of them going into The Mount and bringing Floris out. What Bradley did not tell Victor was the argument Martha and he had had about who that should be.

'I know the place,' Martha said simply.

'Yes and they know you,' Bradley replied.

'Some of them do, but they'd never think I'd come back – simply reappear.'

'Look,' said Bradley, 'not so long ago you didn't even want to leave the Forbidden Territories and now you want to go into the place that scares you the most. I don't understand.'

'*Because* it scares me the most. That's why. I'll tell you what I liked about being Skreech. I had to imagine strengths where I felt I didn't have any. I had to be brave, I had to take chances, I had to be independent. I don't want to stop being these things. Martha is maybe too scared to do this, but Skreech isn't.'

'No,' said Bradley, 'it's too much of a risk. If it goes wrong, you're in the cold room and Floris has lost her chance to escape.'

'But there's so little time. If you take the wrong corridor, if you look as if you don't know what you're doing . . .'

'So tell me all you know and that won't happen.'

Martha sighed a couple of times, pursed her lips and looked at Bradley as if she were measuring him up for the job, then carefully, insistently, she instructed him.

When the lorry passed the next day, Bradley would be on the rise, as close to the edge as possible. There was a sharp incline there and when the driver changed gear, the lorry paused momentarily. That's when Bradley would jump, then pull the bins around him. There shouldn't be many checks on the way in – what would save Bradley was the fact that no one expected anyone to break *into* The Mount.

Bradley slipped over the side of the lorry and crouched behind one of the large wheels. When the driver was inside the building, Bradley went through the door and passed the kitchen. As Martha had thought, the driver and the cook were sitting at the table, before a pot of tea.

Along the same corridor, Bradley found the laundry, as Martha had said he would. It was unlocked. A pile of old grey uniforms lay on the floor. Bradley found one roughly his size, as torn and patched as the others. He crumpled it and rubbed it against the crumbling plaster wall. He didn't want to look anything like the new boy. He put it on and checked none of his clothing was visible. He stood behind the laundry door and took a few deep breaths.

'You've got to move with confidence,' Martha had told him, 'as if you're used to the place, but also to show you have power there. Many inmates come and go. No one knows everyone, but they'll tell if you falter.'

They'll tell if you falter, Bradley told himself. The corridors were long and lit with bare hanging bulbs.

Second on the right, go to the end, there's a big room there, where many of the young ones are – they work on basic technology – that's your best chance.

Bradley swallowed as he approached his 'best chance'. Passing one room, he heard a shout, a slap, a cry.

He peered through the window of the room, at the rows of trestle tables, the bowed heads. Round each table two supervisors prowled. Bradley saw one of them push a child's face towards the machine she was working on, another bend and whisper something, his lip curling as he did so.

Bradley saw Floris three tables from the door. She had her back to him, but he knew it was Floris: her blonde hair, her shoulders shaking with her racking cough. Bradley set his own shoulders back and, with the swagger of a supervisor, he entered the room.

He moved so swiftly, so confidently, neither supervisors nor inmates thought to question his intention.

'Ah, that's the one,' he said, striding up to Floris. She was one of the last ones to turn, her eyes widening as she opened her mouth. Bradley took a clump of her hair in his fist and pulled savagely. Floris screamed with the pain and, as he had seen the supervisor do, Bradley bent his face to her ear, his face a twisted mask of contempt.

'Floris – whatever, you don't know me.'

Bradley loosened his grip but, holding her hair still, he addressed the supervisors.

'Yeah, this is the one Matron wants to see. Complaining about the rations again. Poor little flower.' Bradley forced a laugh and the supervisors joined in. As he pulled Floris up and towards the door, the supervisors aimed half-hearted slaps at her head. She cowered and Bradley understood it was not the first time they had hit her.

In the corridor Floris began to make tiny involuntary mews of nerves.

'It's all right, Floris, we're getting out of here. I've got to hold you like this, though, in case we're seen.'

But the door was in sight. Bradley could see the lorry there, the bins lined up, still to be loaded. Bradley let Floris go and gave her a small smile of encouragement, when out of the kitchen stepped the cook.

She was small and slightly stooped with pinned-back grey hair. She looked at Bradley and Floris and frowned. Bradley knew there was nowhere they could run to.

The cook gave the briefest nod, her hands the smallest calming motion, before she turned back into the kitchen.

'What's the rush?' Bradley heard her say. 'Here, have another biscuit – they're best when they're fresh.'

Quickly, they passed the kitchen door. The second bin lid Bradley lifted showed a bin half-full.

'In here, Floris,' said Bradley and helped her in. 'Keep still and quiet – for however long it takes.'

Bradley found another bin that was not full and climbed into it, hunkering down amid the smell of rotting vegetables.

'Yes, that's fine now,' Bradley heard the cook say. 'Good luck, then,' she added.

'Ah, a trickster of a thing luck is,' said the driver. 'What do I need of luck?'

'Well, good luck to whoever, anyway,' said the cook.

Thanks, said Bradley in the blackness.

The machine ratcheted the bins up onto the trailer and the driver manhandled them into place. The engine kicked into life and the lorry jerked on its way. Bradley heard the gates shut behind him.

The bins shoogled against each other as the lorry drove through the streets to the dump. Bradley could hear the engine sound echo as the lorry entered the narrow streets which led there. It would not be long now.

There was a sudden braking and the bins crashed against each other. Bradley heard the driver's door open and slam, as he got down to remove the broken old park bench from the road.

Bradley pushed the lid from his bin and climbed out, then helped Floris out of hers. It was as Floris was climbing out that he saw them.

'What the—?'

He came round the lorry, his face crimson with fury,

and it was as he was hemmed in between his lorry and the building wall that he came face to face with Hunger.

How he would tell it later, Bradley could not imagine, but he knew the driver's listeners would think he was exaggerating the fierceness of the dog, the black wolf before him, its mad eyes, the glare of its arrow-sharp teeth.

As Hunger held the man at bay – terrified to advance, but equally too scared to turn his back on the monster – Martha and Victor helped Floris down the other side of the truck. She was coughing violently, after her confinement and the enforced silence.

'Floris,' breathed Victor, as they hugged each other. It seemed to Bradley that Victor was standing straighter than he had been since that night when the weasel kidnapped Floris.

Martha frowned at them both. 'Come on, quickly. We need to get away from here. As far away as we can.'

'Right,' said Bradley. 'No going back. We're heading north.'

PART FOUR

NORTH

CHAPTER 13

THE STORM

Bradley smoothed the last of the earth from the turnip and nipped off its trailing root. He held the broad leaves in his fist and snapped them off. He took up the rusted bread knife and half sawed, half pushed his weight down on its blade. One last pressing and the turnip fell open on the earth floor. In the dim light of the barn, it seemed both halves emitted light like twin moons.

Lorry-fall was what they called it. Martha had found its green flag at the roadside bobbing in a pool of snowmelt and rainwater.

Bradley began to cut slices from it, laying each down on its dark rind: preparation, anticipation he knew were part of the pleasure. Already eyes were burrowing into the white flesh, gorging on it.

Bradley laid the knife down and picked up the first slice and handed it to Floris, then another to Victor. Neither had lost their habit of turning away with their food, glancing over their shoulders as they ate.

'Now to the finder.' Martha took hers and ran it backwards and forwards under her nose. Food had been getting scarce lately and she would feed all her senses with this turnip, closing her eyes as finally she crunched into it. Already, Hunger had finished his and was looking for the peel they would soon throw his way.

Last of all, Bradley held out a piece to a large figure which sat slightly beyond the others. The figure inched forward and the light caught the bright scar of a wound over one of his eyes. The brow was still clearly swollen. He took the turnip in his hands, dousing all its light.

'Oh, thank you, my brave boy . . . to be so generous to such a beaten old dog, such a craven mutt as Red Dog has become.'

'Just take it,' said Bradley.

'Oh, indeed yes. But take it with joy in my heart that Red Dog has learned the hard lessons he has and has had the chance to prove what a good and trusted friend he can be.'

There was little stopping Red Dog once he had begun his True Confessions of the Soul – of which this was not the first – so they ate on, concentrating instead on the crunch of the turnip flesh, the sweet juices that filled their mouths, till a low, insistent growl came from Hunger. After Red Dog's weeks of taciturnity, there was something fresh in his wheedling, almost joyful voice this morning that disturbed him. Eventually he turned and snapped in Red Dog's direction. The clack of his teeth briefly put a stop to Red Dog's word play. He lifted the turnip in both hands, as if acknowledging an offering, and bit out a horseshoe from it.

'*Satisfaction Guaranteed.*' He spoke through the pulp.

Martha glared at him.

'Still,' he began again, 'is it not indeed remarkable that here I am who once had such power over one boy soldier, Skreech by name, and now am as but a puppy in the hands of Martha?' He cocked his head and smiled weakly. 'Gentle Martha.'

'Shut it, Red Dog. I've told you, I'm as much Skreech as ever I was.'

'Oh, no doubting, no doubting. The best of both you are. A wonder of the times. And have these times not thrown up one more wonder yet? I speak of Red Dog, the good dog, the Good Samaritan at last.'

Hunger snapped and Red Dog fell silent, absorbed in his turnip, as if it were the most wonderful gift imaginable. Bradley watched him, as he himself gnawed at his turnip skin, and he also thought how unlikely it was that Red Dog should be sitting in their company, sharing their food. So unlikely, in fact, that – not for the first time – he found himself running over in his head the story of how it had come to be.

After they had left the driver of The Mount's refuse lorry, clutching his heart and swearing he would never be the same again, they had loped through the quietest streets of the Invisible City, sticking close to the walls. Martha had begun by leading them, but soon Hunger sensed the direction in which they wished to travel, set the compass inside his head for north and scouted on before them.

When they came to the river on the north side of the Invisible City, it was almost safely dark. They rested again under a bridge till darkness was complete, then set off to cross the ganglands of the Forbidden Territories. Until they cleared the city zones, Bradley had decided it was safer to travel by night.

Martha seemed to have a sixth sense for danger. She knew what would happen to her if she were captured and fear made her always alert. Twice, she managed to pull up short, just when a patrol was about to pass. They had clung to the moonless shadows, Bradley's hand loose around Hunger's jaws.

At other times, Hunger's hearing picked up that, a few streets away, howling boy soldiers were watching some contest or baiting each other and he altered their route accordingly.

Whatever happened, Floris and Victor would not be separated. When the Pack ran across streets that threatened danger, Victor and Floris did so together. And Victor never took so much as a catnap before he was sure Floris was safely sleeping. Her cough tormented her worst at night, but it was a while, after all that had happened, before Bradley realized that it was not simply the cough she struggled to suppress or the fear of flight that had silenced Floris. Sometime in the past miserable weeks, shock had made her mute.

She smiled at Victor nonetheless, who, as they rested, would take risks to bring her back scraps of food – a burnt sausage, a slice of pizza, once even a piece of fruit.

And so, hiding up, sleeping by day and travelling by night, they cleared the violence of the Forbidden Territories of Footrot and Screel and the more ramshackle dangers of the Zones and came to the countryside. Where things were no easier.

At least in the city they could hide – there were walls, old buildings, bridges. It was a world they knew. Sure, there were risks that had to be taken – roads and squares to be crossed. However, these were calculated risks between one place of safety and another and there were many signs for the senses to consult before the start of the smallest journey. But this . . .

They heard the straining engine of another food lorry

and once more cowered in the ditch. They could glimpse it as it approached; imagine its trays of fresh eggs and vegetables, its milk churns, the sacks of wheat from the vast stores of the farm Compounds. But then they had to tuck down their heads as the lorry's chained tyres sent snow spraying over them. No bad thing. The two guards, one riding shotgun in the cabin and the other at the back of the lorry, were always vigilant. Recently, a gang of vagrants had placed spikes in the snow and reared up from the ditch as the lorry spun out of control, its back end lodging in a ditch and its cargo spilling everywhere.

The two guards – who had since received other postings – had seen the hunger and the hate in the eyes of the ragged men who came at them. With wide-armed, help-yourselves gestures, they had disappeared into a barren field. What became of the driver was a mystery.

'OK,' Bradley called, once the engine was a distant buzz. They climbed out of the ditch, brushing off the snow.

He could never get used to this landscape. Even a few minutes in the darkness of the ditch was enough to wash memory of it from him, so that when he climbed out and raised his eyes to it again, he couldn't quite believe it. He could see further than he had ever been able to see in his life – field upon field to the far horizon. It reminded him of his dreams of the sea. At times, he felt he was shrinking – a tiny, insignificant thing that could be stamped on. At others, that he was expanding, like a balloon, to fill the empty space, and in time would surely burst.

Martha and Floris were similarly ill at ease, constantly glancing behind them. But the more they travelled through this countryside, the less there seemed to be behind them – just space, space before them, space behind. Space to fill with their fears.

Of them all, Hunger and Victor felt most at ease. Hunger bounded from the confines of the ditch, Victor close behind him. As they waited for the others – for Bradley, Martha and Floris – to take warily to the road again, Hunger made circles over the lorry's tracks; Victor dipped his hands, running his knuckles over the imprints of the chains. Something was calling to them that, as yet, the others could not hear.

Of course, over the weeks when they had been travelling through it, Bradley was slowly beginning to read the language of this landscape. It was not as flat as he had first imagined. It had hidden shallows and its horizon was not fixed. He soon learned how to read its contours by following the lines of the high wire-meshed fences that enclosed the Compounds. In the centre of these, huge silos gleamed in the winter sun and at night, like ghost ships, the low, eerie lights of the hot-houses marked their place in the darkness. Here tomatoes, grapes, artichokes and melons confounded the seasons.

The farm they would find to take shelter in on the day of the storm could not have been more different.

It began with a few white flakes swirling down from a blue sky. Strangely, it felt warmer than it had done for some days. But then the sky had darkened. Soon it was hidden from them by the unravelling snow. Long, twisting, broken threads of it were whipping into their faces. It was too far to go back to the broken old hut where they had spent the previous night and, besides, how would they ever find it now?

For a while they plodded on – 'Stay close,' Bradley ordered. 'Stay close' – following the deep tracks of the lorries. But soon these were obliterated and Bradley was lifting his eyes into the driving snow, looking for any shape that could give shelter. Oh, for the known terrors of the city now!

Then he saw it, whatever it was – a darkening in the snow. Perhaps it was one of the Compound buildings and a fence lay between them and it. Perhaps they hadn't been travelling north at all, but round in a circle, and this was the first building of the city where all judgements awaited them. Perhaps it was simply a door – a door that would open and, in spite of all their efforts, they'd be brushed away into the nothingness Bradley always worried awaited them. He was wrong to have thought his story might have ended with Red Dog or in The Mount. This was a story he could not remember the Old Woman telling – the door into the dark – yet he must walk towards it and take the others with him: Victor with one arm round Floris, as every so often he dipped his knuckles to the snow to satisfy them both that it would take their weight, and Martha, gripping the edge of Bradley's jacket. Hunger was beside them, then ahead, turning from the storm to assure Bradley that there was a destination worth pursuing.

Bradley stumbled and rose and ploughed on. Glancing up now, he could see the huge door had shape and volume, but no more. The tops of fence posts, like black, upturned heels, guided him off the road towards it.

They dipped their heads and followed him.

Floris screamed. The wind ripped her scream from her and bore it away. A scrap of it reached Bradley, who turned his back on the storm and took the few paces back to where she stood, pointing. Her head had been dipped like the others, but she had turned her face to the side to see, staring at her from the snow, its last hot breath leaving it, a young calf. Perhaps it had escaped from the nearest Compound; perhaps a lorry load of them had come unstuck. Whatever, someone would have questions to answer.

The calf had slipped into the ditch and the snow had drifted against it, supporting it, while making it impossible for it to escape. Both she and it hooded with snow, Floris was the last thing on earth that the calf saw.

Bradley could only nod at her and urge Victor to pull her away. He knew she must be desperately tired. He himself was fighting the desire to lie down on the soft snow and drift into sleep. How had he got to this place, to this terrible tiredness? He felt he had been carrying a huge weight on his shoulders for years.

Already he was on his knees and falling like a tree, a tree whose leafy head was half dreaming. Margaret would be serving tea soon. He would tell her simply to lay the tray down on the thick carpet before the fire. She would see off the dog nipping and pulling at his shoulder, the girl who had slipped a hand under his arm.

At last he would be unencumbered.

'Almost there!' Martha shouted from a long way away and that was all Bradley remembered of that day.

The cold woke him early. For a moment he thought he was back in the basement, back 'home' in the Zone. There was the same shaped darkness, a similarly sharp, earthy smell. Only more so. Then the light hatchings of straw which covered him brought him back to the present moment: to Victor and Floris curled into each other beneath their own nest of straw; to Hunger, who had briefly opened an eye, and to the warmth at his back that was Martha.

Bradley shivered. There was a hard block of ice in his chest that Martha had not been able to melt. He needed to bend his legs, to gather himself into a tight ball of warmth. He hooked his hands behind his knees, but either he was too weak or else his legs were too heavy: he drew short, sharp breaths with the effort. All he needed, he reasoned, was a little more sleep.

Martha was leaning over him, saying, 'We can't travel with you like this. We must stay here another day at least.'

'No, must go now,' said Bradley, and a Bradley of light and of air rose up, leaving the other one – the one made of earth and pain and fever – lying on the barn floor. Bradley watched him go, before he fell again into a dreamless sleep.

He woke searching for his last memory, wondering where he had arrived.

Knives of light sliced through the darkness. Victor rubbed his eyes and pulled Floris closer to him. The minute she woke, he knew her hacking cough would begin.

Hunger's head lifted when he heard the creak of snow-steps outside. He was on his feet and growling low in his throat, when the barn door was pulled open.

Framed against the light, not yet used to the darkness of the barn, the farmer heard a scuffling as Floris took shelter behind Victor. Victor's teeth were bared, glinting like the dog's – the dog, more like a wolf, its hackles up, showing all it had of threat.

The farmer reached for the pitchfork he knew stood by the door. It was braced in his hands when he told them: 'Look, I don't care how many of you there are, you can't stay here. We've little enough to feed ourselves if that's what you're after.'

More spitting. Growling.

'Believe me, I'm keeping nothing from you. There's nothing for vagrants on this farm. You'd best be on your way.'

Bradley looked on from where he lay. Martha was standing now, between him and the man. He knew that if the man kept threatening them with the pitchfork, Hunger would attack him. He imagined Hunger in mid-air, with the twin prongs of the fork plunged into his chest, his own weight impaling him. Victor would be next, spitting and screeching his life away.

Perhaps there was another way this encounter could go, but he could not see it. The man holding back the light had come to cast them all into the world of sleep. Sooner the better.

In the doomed calm, nothing could surprise Bradley, not even when Martha turned on Hunger.

'Hunger. Stop that now. Now.' Her face was close to Hunger's, her eyes locked onto his. Hunger turned his head and glanced down to Bradley and then turned back to Martha. Her eyes had not moved. His growl was like water passing down a drain.

Victor too had quietened, alert to what might happen now. In the silence, there was only Floris's cough.

'Please,' Martha began, 'we mean no harm. But what could we do – lie down and die in the snow?'

'I can't worry about that,' said the farmer. 'There are plenty of ways to perish here and hunger's the one we'll all face if you stay here.'

'We can't leave now,' said Martha. She pointed to Bradley. 'He's not fit to move himself and we can't carry him. If we leave, he stays here and he dies here.'

The man's shoulders slumped, his pitchfork pointed towards the floor.

'But we needn't starve – any of us,' Martha began again. 'Please, come with me. I've something to show you. Hunger, you come too.'

'I'm not saying,' the man said. 'I'm not saying . . . anything . . .'

'I know,' said Martha. 'Just come.'

Outside the sky was high and blue – empty and light. The snow was crisp underfoot.

'Where are you taking me?' said the farmer. But there was little edge to the question, now he had seen that the wolf-dog was the only threat and that this boy or girl – whatever lay beneath all the torn layers – seemed to have control over it. The pitchfork merely steadied him now on the track.

'You'll soon see,' said Martha.

Out in the light, Martha was confirmed in what she had suspected. She saw an old man's sallow face framed by his hat and earmuffs. It was the tremble of panic as much as of anger or threat she had first heard in his voice.

Hunger was sniffing through the thick snow.

'About here,' said Martha and punched through the frozen drift. Her fist found emptiness. A mini avalanche collapsed into the space.

At her fourth punch, her fist jarred against something and when she withdrew it, there they were – a pair of brown eyes staring at her through a film of ice, as they had stared their last at Floris. The eyelashes were like tiny scimitars. Martha excitedly brushed the ice-spicules from the calf's nose and head.

'This should help,' she said, stepping back.

The old farmer's eyes gleamed. 'A calf! A whole calf!' Whether he was trying to dance or simply moved too quickly towards the frozen treasure, he slipped in the snow and fell. As Martha helped him up, he seemed to recollect himself and become suddenly fearful.

'We've got to be careful. Later – we'll do it later.' And

he packed snow back into the hole Martha had made and turned back up the track to the farm.

It was almost dark when they left Bradley sleeping under a mound of straw to return to the calf's snow tomb.

As Victor and Floris stood watch and Hunger surveyed the far horizon, the farmer sliced through the snow with a spade to free the frozen calf. Martha crouched and with her hands dug away snow to clear the hooves. They were bronze in the fading light. She took the end of the rope the farmer passed to her and tied it tightly round its forelegs.

'Often it's the rope that pulls them into the world too,' the farmer said.

They heaved together and with a creak the calf was prised from the snowdrift that had claimed it. The farmer took his spade and collapsed the calf-shaped imprint it had left. He picked up the rope with one hand and began to pull the calf like a sledge. Soon he was panting. Martha took hold of the rope.

'Here,' she said to Victor and Floris, pointing t smooth side of the calf. Victor crouched on it ' yards, drumming his fists on its taut sk skipped off and held Floris's hand as s before she tumbled backwards into t For once, her laugh kept her co

'It's good to hear a youngste

farmer. He looked up into the empty sky; the first stars were clear in it. A light snow was beginning to fall.

'More snow,' said Martha.

'No, just enough to cover our tracks,' said the farmer. 'Winter's had her last big bite at us. The thaw will come soon. You can stay till then.'

'So, what do we call you?'

'Sundep McLachlan. Pleased to meet you . . .'

'Martha.'

That night, when they felt close to sleep, the barn door opened and two figures passed through the moonlit frame, carrying bowls of hot soup. Shreds of meat floated in it and its surface was jewelled with moons of fat. This time, only silence greeted them.

'How's the boy?' said Mrs McLachlan. 'Here, this'll mend him.'

Martha lifted the bowl to Bradley's lips. The hot soup melted a passage of ice through his chest. But before its work was done, Bradley felt the first grains of salt encrusting his lips and he was desperate for a handful of snow to assuage his thirst.

CHAPTER 14

CHLOE

'Bradley. Come in.' Uncle Vince leans against the marble fireplace. Above it, a huge mirror makes the room seem endless. There is no fire in the grate today – only some withered flowers – and, though the sun is dappling the high trees in the valley, inside it is winter. How quickly the seasons pass in these parts! Bradley begins to shiver.

'You will know,' Uncle Vince begins – the 'o' of 'know' like a smoke ring in the chill air – 'that your father left no provision for you. He was blind in more ways than one.' Uncle Vince tugs at a white cuff with pleasure.

Bradley says nothing. He is trying to see the room beyond the room that they are in, reflected in the mirror. Perhaps his mother is in there, wringing her small hands in the lap of her blue dress, waiting to make amends.

'So, what do you have to say?'

Bradley shrugs. 'What does it mean for Chloe and me?'

'It means you're both paupers. It means that your mother and I may support one of you, but certainly not both, given what a pampered creature you've turned out to be.'

Any time now, his mother will come forward and turn on Uncle Vince her blue cut-glass eyes. She will put his world to rights. All will be as it was.

'I am my father's son,' says Bradley. 'I shall have my inheritance.'

'You pip-squeak. You dare to speak to me like that!' Uncle Vince swipes his open hand at Bradley's head. The slap has not toppled Bradley, but his head rings like a bell. 'Out of my sight. Now!'

Bradley turns to the double doors so far away. On the other side of them, he is almost sure, his mother is smoothing down her dress, preparing for an entrance.

He will never know, for he has only started towards them, when the whole room begins to creak like a ship. Both doors burst open, no longer able to hold back a ferocious wind that hits Bradley with such force he must lean low and fight to keep his balance.

The ship pitches now and he slides back a few steps before he is able to re-align his body position to meet this new threat. Furniture topples past him. Amongst it, he counts a studded leather armchair, an inlaid table with iron legs and a cupboard whose feet are four lions' paws. Each could bear him away and crush him against the marble fireplace or into whatever void awaits him. He twists and turns to let them pass.

The brief storm blows itself out and he is returned to an empty room. But the room is vast. And within it he must shield his eyes, for he is almost blinded by blue light: blocks of blue light, stretching out until the far horizon. The wind has drawn tears from his eyes and, as they freeze to his cheeks, he feels the slightest tautness on his skin. Below him, the carpet's intricate design has given way to a carpet of ice that creaks and cracks with each faltering step he takes. But faltering will not save him: he needs to dance to avoid his father's fate.

Uncle Vince's laughter, in the shape of a black bird, passes overhead.

So he dances and dances through the cold and the breaking ice, though his legs burn with tiredness and hunger eats at him. Until he knows only this – he must eat or sleep. Simple choices.

Margaret smiles at him in her old kitchen with its hanging copper pots, its pantry stocked with soup, fruit, oatcakes and . . . and . . . But he fights the dream, knowing, for survival's sake, he must hold onto what is happening. Here. Now.

He crouches on the ice to scratch up a piece of fish-bone, a frill of flesh still frozen to it. He sucks at it, though the bones meld with his lips and take some of his own skin with them when he has finished. Is it the bones that have given him such a raging thirst? Salt surrounds him, encrusts him, courses through him.

Then, through a clear pane of ice, he sees the round brown eyes of a calf staring up at him. It must have slipped from a passing cargo boat. Ice holds its head in place, while its limbs dance below it. Bradley digs at the ice.

The ice shatters over the eyes of the calf. They stare at him blindly, as his father's once did. He is reaching into the blue waters to take the calf's head in his arms, when the platform of ice splinters around him and he falls through it into the icy waters.

Here he knows he needs to wake, wake or be drowned. Only he does not drown, but falls into another room, where he stumbles backwards, till he lands on a hard wooden floor.

And there all the stories he has ever been told dry up.

Bradley holds up his hand and stares at the slow, perfect bead of blood that forms and reforms on the heel of his hand each time after he wipes it. That at least is something real to cling to, as all else seems so unpredictable. For if he lives in a castle, why the broken glass, why the sour smell of alcohol?

Uncle Vince shifts on the burst settee. He has been scratching himself and his hand stays under his armpit, held by his shirt, as he sleeps. Bradley knows not to wake him. He gets up and crunches across the broken glass. In the kitchen he reaches up to open the cupboard doors. They are all empty. He is closing the last door, when he becomes aware of Uncle Vince's breathing in the doorway.

'What is it you're looking for, ya greedy wee pup? Think we can keep you the rate your mother wants to feed you?'

'Where is my mum?'

'Where d'you think? Out with that sister of yours, looking for something to fill you up.'

Uncle Vince yawns and scratches under one arm as he turns. Bradley knows he should not ask the question, knows it riles Uncle Vince, but every so often he can't help himself.

'Dad?'

Uncle Vince spins round. 'Look, you may as well stop asking. He's not coming back. Blind drunk he was, as usual. Wandered off and froze himself to death. Silly bugger. So stop asking. Right?'

Uncle Vince cuffs Bradley round the ear and Bradley stumbles against the cupboard. Inside, the cups chink against each other.

'Careful!' says Uncle Vince.

Bradley remembers his father before blind-drunkenness, before the Dead Time. Bradley was very small then and his father could throw him up in the air. Bradley remembers hanging there a long time, like a star in the sky.

'You're my little star,' his father would shout. And Bradley would look down on his father's smooth face, his shining eyes, his bright white shirt. But this was a long time ago, when he had a name that was never spoken now, though he strained to hear it. All he could make out was a crash of consonants and vowels that sounded like a curse.

The door opens and Bradley's mother and sister, Chloe, come in. His mother has a plastic bag in her hands. Uncle Vince grunts an enquiry her way.

'Some potatoes,' she says. 'A bone.'

'A bone,' Uncle Vince sneers. 'D'you think we're dogs? Huh, probably not as well off, eh. What else? What else?'

'I got it, if that's what you're asking,' says Bradley's mother. She looks up at Uncle Vince. Her blue eyes are grey and red-rimmed, her cheeks pinched.

'Right, fine. But watch that tone with me. I'm the one that's keeping a roof over our heads, remember – though for how long I can manage that . . . Here, give me it.'

Bradley's mother takes out the bottle and hands it

over to Uncle Vince. It is a clear liquid, like water, but still it makes him cough.

Chloe and Bradley watch him take a couple more long gulps. What will happen? He may hug them and cry. He may look at Bradley and become suddenly angry.

Their mother is watching too – like a hawk.

'A little bit, please. Just a swallow or two . . .'

Uncle Vince looks at her in disgust. This is a recent request, but one she makes with more and more urgency.

'Please, sweetheart.'

'Pah!' says Uncle Vince and thrusts the almost empty bottle into her outstretched hands.

Soon now, their mother will take to the bed she shares with Uncle Vince, turn her face to the wall and weep helplessly, her greasy hair spread out across the dirty pillow.

'Where are you two going?' Uncle Vince asks. 'Sit down where I can keep my eyes on you – before you eat us out of house and home.'

They sit by the fireside, nursing the dying fire, as Uncle Vince's red eyes grow more and more malevolent, before finally they close and he tips over into sleep.

Chloe takes Bradley by the wrist.

'Come on,' she says. 'We're going on an adventure.'

She brings a blanket from under their mother's bed and tells Bradley to put on all the clothes he has – another pair of socks, a jersey, his padded top.

'Sshh,' she says, as she opens the door and waves him into the street. The door shuts on Uncle Vince's grunting sleep, their mother's fitful weeping.

The streets are quiet, but Chloe knows where she is going and needs no one to guide her. The streets all look the same to Bradley. Smashed windows, spray-painted walls, eyes in empty doorframes.

After an age – or so it seems to Bradley – they come to a street of old shops with broken signs.

'Here,' says Chloe. 'Let's rest in this doorway.'

'Yes,' says Bradley. His short legs are tired now and it is good to have a blanket wrapped around him and to share his sister's warmth.

'You remember,' Chloe says – then there is a name, but it is all vowels, soft and indistinct – 'when Mummy and I go out? You know where we get most of our food?'

Bradley shakes his head.

'People give it to us. We sit with our hands out and kind people give us food. Shall we try that tomorrow?'

'Yes, please,' says Bradley. He is so hungry he can hardly wait till tomorrow – one short sleep away.

'Good,' says Chloe. 'Good.' Then there is that vowelly word again, but even softer now. And again. It is almost like the sound of sleep itself.

* * *

When Bradley wakes up the next morning, he is in the doorway alone. He waits for Chloe, but she does not come back and he cannot remember the way home.

With hunger comes the memory of what Chloe had told him to do. This seems as good a place as any. He puts out his hands.

Soon – 'Poor wee boy' – 'Too young to be living like that' – 'Ach, another one' – he has collected almost more bread and scraps than he can eat himself. Then he sees, coming towards him, yellow eyes glinting in the midday light, a huge, sharp-eared dog . . .

Martha stroked Bradley's forehead. Yet another bowl of soup had gone cold – its surface yellowy and thick-skinned. Hunger licked his lips.

Bradley had been turning and muttering in his sleep for two days now. 'Whatever's troubling him – that's it coming out,' said the farmer's wife. 'Don't fret, Martha. He's mending. Suffering, but mending.'

Then Bradley's eyes opened and fixed on Martha's face. The words were strange, but he said them to Martha as if they would make perfect sense to her. Twice.

'Chloe. Chloe is my princess.'

CHAPTER 15

THE LAKE

Sundep McLachlan had been right. It didn't snow again after that last flurry. And the snow that had fallen formed a crust over itself that grew more and more fragile and crystalline. Below it, the seeds split and their shoots began to push towards air and light.

The old farmer was as good as his word. After they had shown him the entombed calf, there had been no argument about them staying there. He and his wife even encouraged them to wash and to patch their clothes. With more persuasion, they allowed Mrs McLachlan to cut their matted hair. Floris and Victor rarely left the barn – 'That cough'll never clear up with winter here,' said Mrs McLachlan. 'Best stay inside as long as you can.'

Somehow, in his captivity, Victor had managed to

hide Floris's blue glass and now it was returned to her, she lay content for hours, turning it against the light; through its tiny portal entering her magic world.

Martha and Bradley helped around the farm as much as they could – repairing fences and broken gates. But it was dangerous for them to be seen, so they found themselves living a life much as they had in their Zone. The barn became for them, as their basement had been, part refuge, part prison. Helping was for them a release and the McLachlans were good teachers.

'Hold it this way,' Sundep McLachlan instructed Martha on how to wield a hammer. 'Now, nice and steady . . . That's the stuff, you've got the hang of it now.'

'Come on,' said his wife to Bradley, 'and I'll show you how to make that soup that's so good for you.'

In the kitchen she took two shrivelled onions from the back of a cupboard and began to slice them. She stopped after the first one and stroked her cheek with the back of her hand.

'What do I do?' Bradley asked.

'Oh, nothing. Just watch. It's good to have a boy beside me when I cook . . .' She tucked a strand of grey hair behind an ear and smiled at him.

'We used to have a boy, you see – a fine boy. He'd work all day for his father, then stand and tell me all about it while I was cooking. Thought he was helping me, he did. And he was. He was.'

'What was his name?'

'Sundep, like his father. Young Sundep. And we had a good farm for him to take over – and he wanted nothing different.'

'What happened to him?'

'Oh, for a long time nothing but good things. He grew up, tall like his father, but with more sense of fun. He was always making people laugh – me most of all! But not only me – the men who worked on the farm too, and the neighbours. And most of all the girls.'

Bradley frowned.

'You should laugh more, you know. Something about you around the eyes reminds—'

'Laugh at what?'

'Yes, you're right and, huh, here's me talking . . .'

'So what happened?'

'Simple. He fell for one of the local girls – someone he'd grown up with from the nearest farm. But you know how girls can change.'

'Yes. That is, no . . . not really.' Bradley thought Mrs McLachlan wouldn't be thinking of girls like Martha.

'Well, take it from me. One minute some of them can't bear to be beside a boy and the next . . .'

'What?'

'It's very different. Anyway, young Sundep married her and they both came and lived here. For a while it was the happiest time. She was like the daughter we'd never had and young Sundep – oh, to see a son so happy!'

'And?'

'And then what should have been the happiest time became the saddest. She became pregnant – a grandchild for us – then the Dead Time hit us. But we got through it somehow. It was the aftermath that did for us. We lost most of our land and all our animals to the Compounds. That first year, before we learned what you could do with roots and berries, before we learned to plan and to preserve, we survived on scraps. Everything was rationed. We watched each other getting thinner and thinner . . . and though we all made sacrifices, gave up our own food for the baby, he got weaker and weaker. When he should have been toddling, he sat on the floor and stared up at his mother with huge, empty eyes. When winter came, nothing could save him. His mother, who'd been a girl just two winters before, looked middle-aged now. Young Sundep cursed the land. They told us they could not stay here, there was nothing for them but painful memories. So they left for the city to try their luck there.'

Bradley had heard the stories of starvation in the north that kept everyone in the Zones. 'Nothing for anybody out there,' people said. 'If you think this is bad . . . At least there's shelter and the chance of a meal now and again, if you're clever enough, eh?'

'Of course, we've never heard from them again. But being followers of the Faith keeps us going.'

'The Faith? What's that?'

'It's what we believe. *What has been lost will be found. Those who give will have their gifts passed on.*'

'I don't understand.'

'Well, many of us in the Faith have lost children – to the Compounds, to the Zones; some have even gone to the forests of the north. We believe that if we take in whoever knocks on our doors, that hospitality will be passed on to our children wherever they are.'

'Are there many of you?'

'No, very few. All of us live in farms starved by the Compounds. But you're lucky that you came to a farm of the Faith. Any other, you would have had a far harsher welcome. You could have been shot or handed over to the Compounds to be taken back to the Zones – or worse. You see, whether he wanted to or not, Sundep had to take you in. For young Sundep's sake. For his sake, if for no other.'

Mrs McLachlan's hands lay inert on the chopping board. She stared out of the window a long time before Bradley left the room.

The closer they got to spring, the hungrier they got. The snow was lying in patches now around the countryside – like a giant half-finished jigsaw.

'Give it two weeks,' Sundep McLachlan said. 'I don't know what the road north will be like – no one dares go there now – but the thaw could flood it or mud could make it impassable.' And it was true that they could hear the food lorries revving their engines as the mud held them on the road into the city.

But they couldn't stay inside for ever – their hunger wouldn't let them. Martha and Bradley began to explore the land that lay behind the farm, far from the road. The farmer had told them of a small lake that was surrounded by hazel trees, hidden by a small rise.

'There used to be fish in it,' he said. 'But these days I'd not like to say. I'd get up to it myself if I could. Still, if you could catch us one, that would be a fine thing.'

Hunger ran on ahead or made large looping explorations around them. It was good to see him stretch his legs in an open space and flow over the fields. But this was a new Hunger for Bradley. And he was still missing the old one. Since Bradley's fever, Hunger was as likely to follow Martha as he was Bradley.

He would respond to Bradley's commands as readily as ever, but he talked only in the dog's way – with barks or whines or with the angle of his head. The deep, equal understanding between them seemed to have gone. Bradley missed it. As he watched Hunger run so magnificently, he felt again jealous of what he had lost; for he had his suspicions.

'Martha?'

'What?'

'Does Hunger ever . . .'

'Ever what?'

'You know . . . ?'

'Not unless you tell me, I don't.'

'Ever, well, like . . .'

'Like what, Bradley? Ask the question!'

'Does Hunger ever *talk* to you?'

'*Talk* to me . . . ?' Martha's tone and her face spoke equally of her astonishment. 'As in, "How are you today, Martha?"'

'No, not quite – you know what I mean.'

'I haven't a clue what you mean! Though just this morning he did ask if I didn't think you were getting a little odd.'

She looked at Bradley and the wildness of his question finally struck him.

'And how did you answer?' he said.

'I said, "Yes, Hunger, he thinks you're talking to him."'

Martha laughed and Bradley just caught her laughter – her face uplifted to the light, her eyes dancing – before he joined in, laughing as much out of relief as anything. Laughter – he felt it tugging at his chest. Then Hunger was there, snaking between them, and they both crouched down and hugged him so closely they were also hugging each other's arms, so closely their cheeks touched.

They drew apart and Martha looked at Bradley, cocking her head slightly like a dog. Her eyes flicked in tiny movements around his face, never leaving it, taking in each part of it, as you would wish to know the face of someone who had just saved you from a burning building or a prison cell.

'Bradley Prince,' she said. 'Bradley Prince.'

'That's my name.'

And the last splinter of ice in his chest finally thawed.

They followed the track through the stunted hazel trees and came to the lake's shore. It was a small lake, yet the water was as blue as the sky. Bradley felt warmth on his face for the first time that year.

But Hunger had frozen, his ears alert, his nose pointing.

Along the shore there was a wisp of smoke. Close by it, out in the lake, the water's surface was ruffled.

Bradley touched Martha's arm and they crouched down behind the last line of hazels. They crept along behind the trees, till they could see a pile of clothes and the glint of a fish lying beside the fire.

The surface of the lake exploded.

A huge figure rose from it – pulling the water with it – holding a fish like a wriggling bar of light in its hands. The figure appeared to kiss the fish, then to dance out of the water with it. He tapped its head twice against one of the stones around the fire and laid it beside the other one.

They had come across the occasional vagrant before, though after the ambush of the food lorry the gangs had migrated elsewhere. In this live-and-let-live world they had given each other a wide berth.

But this was no ordinary vagrant. Bradley recognized immediately the broad naked torso, the perfectly bald head and hairless face. And so did Martha. *Once met, never forgotten.* Turning to her, Bradley saw her face bulk and harden round the edges, as briefly she put on Skreech again.

They watched as Red Dog stamped his feet, swung his arms, then turned back into the water. As he dipped below the surface, Martha and Bradley nodded grimly to each other. Was it safe to pretend they had not seen him, so close to the McLachlans as he was? They looked around – the biggest sticks of wood they saw would be as twigs to Red Dog.

Bradley felt a cage forming in the air around him. He reached out a hand and touched Martha's arm to prove to himself that he still could. He was aware her breathing had quickened. With their eyes fixed on Red Dog, neither Bradley, Martha nor Hunger noticed the movement of branches at the fringe of the wood, where it was closest to Red Dog's fire.

Claw stooped beneath a hazel branch and stepped down the banking onto the stony lakeshore. His left knee clicked yet again, like two stones knocking into each other. Still, at least this time it had not locked. He wondered whether he had another winter left in him. His joints seemed to take it in turns to give him pain.

He rubbed the stiffness from his neck and craned his head from side to side. He took in what he saw with his own narrowed eyes and looked for what they missed with the blind hollows of the wolf's head he wore above his own.

No one but the fisherman.

He took another few steps towards Red Dog's fire, turning his head this way and that, sifting through the smoky air. He was broad-backed, bow-legged, and his grey hair flowed over the wolf-skin he wore round his shoulders.

He gave a low whistle and the others came out, blinking in the sunlight. Bradley, wide-eyed, counted two more men, two women and three children. One was a baby tied to its mother's back. They were all partly dressed in animal skins. The first man was the only one with a headdress, though the two younger men carried clubs – stones the size of fists, tied into split wooden shafts.

Empty bellies had drawn them once more far from the depths of the forest. Claw had smelled the fire and led them to this spot. How long they would survive without him, he could not guess. The younger men could be ferocious, no denying that, but to be wolf was also to listen to the forest; to smell the forest; to fill your eyes with the forest. To use whatever wisdom a brutish life allowed. The mothers at least knew that.

Claw signalled to them that they should stay by the fire. To the two children he spoke firmly, raising his fist as if he might strike them. They needed to be bold to survive in the forest; but more, they needed to learn. Perhaps this giant would be prepared to share with them, yet he was a new and unpredictable challenge. Whatever happened, the children, tucked in behind the wolf men, would be safe.

Red Dog was gone a long time – or so it seemed to those who watched and waited in the silence – before, his cavernous chest almost airless, he leaped up from the water. His arms were raised over his head, a trout was in his fist – and there was only a narrow strip of water between him and the wolf men. They appeared to laugh at him – or to grimace – as Red Dog lost control of the trout and juggled with it, before the fish fell back into the water and skimmed away below its surface. Momentarily, his forehead had lifted in the openness of shock. Now it came down into the helmet Bradley and Martha had known so well.

He shouted a challenge, his breath pluming in the cold air. Claw answered by opening his arms wide to include the giant, his own company, and the fire and the fish. But again came the unmistakable challenge. Claw shrugged his shoulders. Long ago he had decided not to stand in the way of whatever fate had in store for him.

The younger men, though, hissed and moved from foot to foot, cupping their club-heads in their hands. While Claw's own wolf was old now, as he was, and moved round as carefully, their wolves still seemed caged within them. The young men felt a battering on their ribcages, as howls sounded in their ears and their eyes glared with violence.

From the fireside, the women looked on impassively.

Red Dog filled his barrel chest with air; emptied it and filled it again. As he did so, his shoulders opened and he pulled the sledgehammers of his fists up level with them. Like a great bear, he set off, roaring, towards the three wolf men who confronted him. Water sprayed all around him, but never reached his enormous naked chest.

Watching him, Martha could not quell a grudging admiration. She recalled how safe he had made Skreech feel those first nights. To the damaged girl she was, he was all-powerful, worthy of her trust. The worst thing back then had not been his threats, but his crocodile tears.

'Oh my boys, if you only knew how I worried about you; if you only knew what a weight of responsibility I feel. Oh, this harsh, cruel world . . .'

He never cleared the water.

While he had galloped, raging, his eyes were fixed on the two blind pools above Claw's head. Below his sightline, the first boy-child, ducking low, had brought a sharp-edged stone in a great arc, crashing into his knee. His momentum allowed Red Dog two further, halting steps, before he fell like a toppled tree, face first into the water. With one last yelling lunge, his clubbing fist struck the other child, sending him hurtling into the shallows. Not finished yet, by a long way.

But as he writhed to raise himself, they were on him. A club landed above one eye; another finished him with two blows from behind. Blood oozed into the clear waters of the lake.

With another slight shrug, Claw turned and they left Red Dog beached in the shallows, the water settling around him.

Bradley and Martha saw the blood lust leave each other's eyes. They had lived each swing of the axe. Both had struggled to contain Hunger's urge to join the attack and to howl victory. Now, though, he seemed to accept the moment had passed and was calm.

The wolf men stooped to wash the blood from their clubs. Claw spoke to the child who had been struck and helped him back to the fire. The women skewered sticks into the fish and held them over the flames. The injured child would be fed flakes of fish from the arthritic hand of the wolf leader himself.

As they waited for the fish to cook, the smaller woman suckled her baby. The others sat on their haunches, staring across the water of the lake. Claw looked down on the struck child, reaching his fingers under his headdress to scratch his scalp. *Let me give the boy my next winter*, he thought. *And the next. And the one after that, till he is strong enough for the life we must live.*

Bradley and Martha's interest was not in the wolf folk. They watched only to see whether Red Dog had truly been vanquished. They turned to each other and again nodded. Two pairs of eyes had not been deceived. Red Dog had not moved.

But Hunger was not to be denied honouring this victory. His two barks were short and shrill.

Time froze. The wolf folk turned their heads from the fire and stared back into the hazel wood. It seemed that the world held its breath for an age, as Bradley and

Martha, muzzling Hunger, tried to become one with the hazel trees, and the wolf folk listened to what the hazel trees could tell.

Bradley dared not turn to Martha, dared not move a muscle, till he heard her breath in a long, slow exhalation, followed by his own.

With a signal from Claw, the baby was tied again onto its mother's back, the struck child lifted to his feet. The wolf folk moved again, silently and warily as they had come, back into the wood.

'Come on,' said Bradley. 'We've seen enough.'

Bradley and Martha knew not to tell Victor and Floris about Red Dog and how he had met his fate. Their agitation would have been too great even to know Red Dog had come so close. So it was that Victor's and Floris's shock was the greater when they saw through the McLachlans' kitchen window the monstrous shadow of Red Dog filling out a chair, as Mrs McLachlan cleaned his head wounds with a cloth from a basin of reddened water.

Floris put her hand to her mouth and let out a silent scream. Victor crouched his fists to the ground to steady himself, a high-pitched keening cutting through the cold air.

Neither would leave the barn with Bradley to check whether what they had seen was a ghost.

'You saw him!' Victor said. 'You saw him. Didn't tell Victor. Didn't tell Floris.'

'We thought he was dead.'

'Dead. Dead. *Is there. Is himself.* All the big of him. The bully of him.'

That was not the picture Red Dog presented to Mrs McLachlan when she challenged him with his history. Through the window, Bradley saw his forehead lift and settle, lift and settle, as shock mixed with calculation.

'He's an injured man, badly injured,' Mrs McLachlan argued with Bradley and Martha afterwards. 'You *know* I couldn't turn him away. He barely made it to the gate, half naked and drenched with blood. He has brought firewood and fish and potatoes he wants to share with you as a peace offering.'

'Peace offering!' Bradley said.

'He denies nothing, but claims he was a protector in hard times who has changed. Believe me, he's no threat to anyone.'

'You can't say that,' said Martha. 'You can never say that.' But she had insisted she would face him with Bradley. See him, eye to eye, in his defeat. As long as Hunger was with her.

'Red Dog,' said Bradley. It was an accusation.

'Ah, bless me . . . No . . . Well yes, who used to be

Red Dog sits before you in his shame, but not the Red Dog you knew.'

'No?' said Martha.

'Oh no, not that one, my dear Skreech, I thought you were—'

'Save it, Red Dog,' spat Martha.

'Yes, yes, but let me . . . As I was saying, not that Red Dog. But one who has had the worst of times and seen all the errors of his ways. One who delights – yes, *delights* is not too strong – in seeing those he can make things right with sent before him now.'

'Never,' said Bradley.

'Oh, never is such a long time, my friends.'

'We're not your "friends" – and I'm not Skreech.'

'Well, you're the ghost of him if you're not.'

'My name's Martha.'

'Martha, Martha, is it really? Good lord, all this time. What a blind old dog Red Dog's been in more ways than one. But what stories we've got to tell.'

'Stories? Pah,' said Martha.

'Stories,' said Red Dog. Bradley and Martha looked at each other.

'I mean, what harm can Red Dog be? Look at him, in the dock before you, wearing nothing but his shame.'

True, with his face wounds fresh, his head bandaged, Red Dog looked shorn of his former menace. Inquisitiveness got the better of them both.

Red Dog squatted over the kitchen grate. No finger of smoke got past him. Every so often the fire spat as a drip of fat from the fish fell from the skewer.

'Oh, nice fish, lovely fish. Fish for my . . . sometime, perhaps, who knows? . . . my friends . . .' Red Dog chanted at the fish. He poked around in the embers with a twig and skewered a potato.

'Please,' he said, 'sit, eat. There's lots more potatoes in there. Show a bit of trust to an old dog.'

'Yeah, sure,' said Bradley. But the smell of the fish and the creamy innards of the potato Red Dog had broken open – with a laugh at his black, burnt fingers – proved too inviting.

'Just one trick . . .' Bradley said. And perhaps Hunger still picked up the odd word or two, for he began to growl with renewed force.

'Oh, Red Dog's done with tricks. No tricks left. Absolutely trickless, is Red Dog. But here, please let me at least give a potato to the champion there. He looks as if he's about to tear me to shreds.'

'Yes,' said Bradley, growing in confidence with Hunger's steady, snarling display. 'Hunger doesn't forget. Just one trick, remember . . .'

'On my poor, misbegotten, miserable life, I swear. Besides, wouldn't you relish hearing the story of Red Dog's calamitous fall?'

Red Dog lifted the fish from the fire just in time, for

the flesh simply fell off the bone. They picked it up with their fingers – white, sweet flakes of it. They wanted to shut their eyes to taste it the better, to hear only the sound of the fire and of Hunger crunching the head and the bones, but they dared not take their eyes from Red Dog.

And the potatoes! They came out of the fire like black cannonballs but, once split, they released a rush of steamy pleasure.

'Where did you get these potatoes, Red Dog?' Martha asked.

'Oh, ask me no questions and I'll tell you no lies.' Red Dog touched a forefinger to his nose. He almost seemed to be enjoying their company. 'Oh, here's another one,' he said, just when they thought they were all gone. He juggled with it – 'Oh! Oh! Oh!' – then threw it lightly to Martha.

'Room for one more?'

As they turned the potato skins inside out and licked into the crevices, the white veins of flesh, before tossing the empties to Hunger, Red Dog stared into the grey ashes of the fire and told them his story.

The night Hunger had defeated the Hound of Hell should have been the crowning glory of Red Dog's power struggle with Black Fist. Instead it had been the night his world had begun to fall apart.

It wasn't the fact of the supposed chemicals that had

blunted the Hound's fighting prowess. The powers that be were not interested in these little spats. In fact, they encouraged competition between those whose destinies they controlled. Black Fist's complaints to the Invisible City might have been swept aside altogether, if it were not for the fact that they were linked to the escape of Red Dog's captives. And if these had simply been absorbed by a rival gang in the Forbidden Territories or had scampered back to the Zone from which they evidently had come, well then, there would have been no cause for anything but mild amusement among those in the Invisible City.

But matters were more serious than that. The security of the Invisible City itself had been breached. The escapees had broken into The Mount and stolen a valuable worker. Such things could not be allowed to happen. Black Fist's complaints were upheld. More, they were backed up by the weasel – 'My very own *Loot-tenant*' – who'd become Black Fist's second in command. Red Dog was finished.

'So what happened?' asked Bradley.

'Well, there's no court of appeal at the Invisible City,' said Red Dog. 'That's what's invisible about it. Not the buildings or the people who live there, but the power. The power guards itself through its invisibility and the whole city takes its name after it. Clever, eh? Too clever by half for poor old Red Dog.'

'So what happened?' Martha took up Bradley's question. She wanted the whole story from Red Dog. She wanted to feel his story; to weigh the truth of it; to see how far, if at all, he could be trusted.

'Simple really,' said Red Dog. 'The Invisible City wouldn't trade with me any more. The word got out to everyone. And all those poor souls – those defenceless children, of whom once you, Skreech— Martha, begging your pardon, was one – had their guide and protector made powerless, as powerless as you see him now.'

'So?' said Bradley.

'So they left me. Each and every one. No choice, they said – if they dared say anything to me before they left. They went to Black Fist – Black Fist and that ungrateful wretch. It didn't happen at once of course. First, it was a drift. Then the discipline went. And without discipline . . . I became simply a figure of mockery for them. Black Fist let it be known it wouldn't be safe for me to stay around, so one night I fled – fled in the only direction I could. North.

'And here you have found me. So if you want to mock old Red Dog, mock him. If you want to stick red-hot sticks into him, do so. For Red Dog can run no further. It is up with him. If you cannot believe change has entered an old dog's heart, then let my end be here – and let those who have brought me the light of humility be the ones to do it.

'But for Mrs McLachlan's sake, for the sake of young Sundep and all his memory means to these fine folk, perhaps you'll give a sinner a chance. And if you do, I'll promise to keep out of your way, till my debt to these Good Samaritans is paid.'

Bradley and Martha both harrumphed, the closest they could get to a believe-it-when-we-see-it position. But there was nothing – not potato skins or sweet flakes of fish – that would buy the trust of Victor or Floris. Floris scurried to the furthest corner of the barn, while Victor growled and spat at Red Dog whenever he came near.

There was a small field beside the farm. 'It's where we grow stones,' Mr McLachlan said.

'For the stone soup?' said Red Dog.

'That'll be it,' said Mr McLachlan, thinking, yes, he could see why children would be scared of this man, but there was nothing wrong with his sense of humour.

He had always meant to clear the field; felt that without the stones it would be possible to till and to plant it with something that wouldn't demand too much of the earth, a hardy strain of cabbage perhaps. The small stones he could rake off himself – in fact, tell a lie, these children had already cleared most of them – but the others, the ones that had been rooted there for ever and a day, he could barely bend down to, never mind shift.

Red Dog gave a leave-it-to-me nod and set to work. He crouched till the skirts of his black coat brushed the ground as he moved. He set his hands to work, each independent of the other, plucking the stones from the earth, one by one, as if they were ripe. Any that refused to come first time broke his rhythm, but spiked his interest. He turned to them his full attention, excavated them with both hands and gave each a respectful nod, before he tossed it onto one of the random cairns forming round the edge of the field.

Each morning he cast his eye over the field and blew on his hands. Still the field challenged him, but he knew there would be only one victor here. Nor was Red Dog unaware of his audience. From the kitchen window, Mr McLachlan pointed him out again to his wife.

'What a worker that is. I've rarely seen the like.'

And from round the edge of the barn and through its slats, Bradley and the others watched too, as Red Dog dug his hands into the earth to allow him handholds on a rock like a giant submerged egg. After the first two or three days there were no easy ones left. As Red Dog heaved now, they saw the seams of his coat ease apart, as the rock lifted slowly up and up, till eventually it toppled over and its black, earthy back faced the sky, leaving another smooth empty socket in Mr McLachlan's new field.

But one stone above all proved the greatest test. It sat

dead centre of the field and Mr McLachlan had imagined, when he came to plant the field, that he would have to work around it.

Red Dog threw his coat over the nearest cairn and rolled up the sleeves of his shirt. He walked over to the stone, still limping slightly, with a fence post resting over his shoulder. He raised it above his head and drove it into the earth. A splinter pierced his palm, but he merely pulled it out and sucked the bleeding away. He muttered at the stone. It was almost as if he were amused by what had happened. But when the fence post broke, his helmet-brow furrowed with thought. He strode off to the barn and, smiling his grimacing smile into the curious shadows, he lifted a crowbar down from the wall.

He spat on his hands and drove the crowbar into the earth beside the giant stone. And that was when the black rains began, with no pitter-patter of warning, but straight and hard. Within seconds they had filled up each of the field's fresh cavities. Red Dog shook his head and turned his back on the stone and pushed down upon the crowbar with all his strength. He was facing the barn, so even through the inky rain Bradley could not miss how he strained, his forehead peeling back till the blind white slits of his eyes stared back at Bradley and every nerve mapped his hairless face, as if some force inside him were trying to escape. The steady hum of his effort became so great, Hunger heard it in the shelter of the barn and padded, whining, backwards and forwards.

As Red Dog's blood vessels pulsed beneath the rods of rain, his head bandage began to unwind and to trail down his back. But he did not stop work then, or when fresh blood bubbled up from the wounds and rivulets of rain and blood poured down his neck, across his shoulders and down the prow of his chest. Once he caught sight of Mr McLachlan stepping out beyond the shelter of the eaves, but he turned to him the closed helmet of his face and stopped him in his tracks.

Again and again, the beast of a stone lifted and fell. And again and again, Red Dog wiped his hands beneath his armpits and set to work, humming and growling; till, against the dying light, with a bent crowbar, he cancelled the stone's dead weight – 'Gotcha!' – and rolled it to the side of the field. Mr McLachlan was there to praise him, to share a joke with him, he thought, about the newly-stopped rain; but Red Dog merely gave him the same nod he had at the beginning of the work, as if it had been nothing, and muttered, 'Satisfaction guaranteed.'

'What a worker. I've rarely seen the like.'

'Asks about the children too,' said Mrs McLachlan. 'Did I not tell you the Faith repays its followers?'

For almost two weeks Red Dog became a man of few words as, exhausted, he slept each night on an old sack in the barn, curling into his coat, steam rising from his warming body, his boots still coated in mud. Hunger lay between the Pack and him. No one settled to sleep till they saw Red Dog's body heave with deep even breaths and heard his snores.

Even so, Bradley found himself wondering, could it be possible that Red Dog had not been lying; that he had truly changed?

'Well,' said Bradley, tossing his turnip skin towards Hunger, 'we can't live on lorry-fall for ever. Today, we carry on north.'

Floris looked at Victor nervously. She shook her head vigorously.

'Stay,' said Victor, speaking for her. But there was a gleam in his eyes that said yes.

'We can't,' said Bradley. 'There's no food and there's no reason. The snows have gone. The floods have eased. We must go north.'

Floris cuddled into Victor.

'And it's not safe here any more,' said Martha. 'We can't stay in the barn the whole summer and the Compound patrols will surely spot us if we spend more time outside. We can't go back to the city . . .'

Victor's eyes widened in alarm.

'. . . We have no choice but to head north.'

'North,' said Victor.

Floris slowly nodded.

'Good,' said Bradley.

'Wise children. Oh, good and wise children,' said Red Dog.

They agreed that Red Dog could accompany them part of the way – to the last Faith house before the forests began. Mr McLachlan told of a poor couple there who would welcome the labour.

'Anything,' Red Dog said. 'Anything to help.'

Floris and Victor had both needed convincing about this agreement. Martha had had to point out to them all the things Red Dog had done to show how he had changed. There was the work he had done for the McLachlans for a start. And he had gone to the lake and brought them fish, returning cold and damp. He had caught a rat, sniffing around Floris as she slept. His hand had whipped out in the darkness like a snake's head. They had seen him bend at the waist every time Mrs McLachlan came near and talk about the weather and about how Floris and Victor were growing, what fine young people were Bradley and Martha, but yes, how one worried about what future they could have in these times. Oh, before the Dead Time . . . And Mrs McLachlan's face would cloud. They never talked about life before the Dead Time, but people rarely did. Still, she was thankful the children would have some kind of protector with them, for part of the journey at least, as they headed north, where for so long no one had dared to go.

CHAPTER 16

REVENGE

Red Dog's tall figure, with its huge boots and short trouser-cuffs, was the last one Sundep McLachlan and his wife had seen as they took the road that led north of the farm before, after a small rise, it dipped from view.

There was a track which ran to the side of the road, though the road itself was markedly narrower now than the one they had taken out of the city. The track was rougher than the road, but there were protective bushes on either side of it, some showing tiny, arrowed leaves.

Spring was in the air and Red Dog felt his time had come.

If he raised himself up fully, he could see Dog Boy in the lead, forging steadily ahead, the bag of food Mrs McLachlan had given them for the journey bouncing on his back. Victor and Floris came next. Victor leaned towards the ground and every so often reached down to brush the earth with the knuckles of a hand. He tugged at Floris to keep up.

Then came Skreech. Skreech – the cause of all his problems.

Falling away a little behind them, Red Dog could let his lip curl at the thought of her name, as he had not been able to do these past weeks, when 'Martha' had to be said so sweetly. For every sweet saying of the name won Bradley over, bit by bit. Any fool could see that.

But his quarrel was not with 'Martha'; it was with Skreech. Not for the deception. He had had his suspicions – many girls found it safer to become boy soldiers than to stay with families and watch hunger and despair seize them. Everyone was playing a part to get by.

Red Dog ran the case against Skreech one last time through his mind.

Dog Boy, Victor and Hunger, *his* champion – Red Dog had held them all within his power back then. And he had had the beating of Black Fist – a victory that would have engraved his name in the minds of all throughout the Forbidden Territories and, more importantly, in the Invisible City itself.

Red Dog felt his chest fill with his old power, but it was only the ghostly power of what might have been. It soon passed from him, leaving him shrunken, breathless.

Skreech's treachery had done this to him. Skreech, whom he had taken in as a fearful little boy with a voice like a broken whistle. Given him shelter, food, given him his protection. Trusted him. And how had Skreech repaid him? By abetting his enemies, by setting him on the road to humiliation, to cold, to hunger, to fear.

Fear? Red Dog afraid! Yes, he had been. The great shape of him trying to scurry like a mouse, like a shadow, through the Invisible City with the few necessities he had been able to take with him on his back. Unnatural.

He stretched himself now and felt his shoulders unwrap and his chest open to the future like a bulging wardrobe. As he savoured his justified anger, he felt his forehead crease and resettle like a helmet on his head.

For there had been no end to his humiliations these past weeks. He had had to become not only Red Dog of the soft voice, but of the open face, of the bright comment also. He had found lifting rocks was preferable to spending any more time than he had to like that; and he would rather lift rocks from a hundred fields than taste again the milky skin of that old woman's cheek as he had kissed her goodbye. He could feel his lips pucker with distaste. Enough!

Skreech had been false from the start and now Skreech – he, she or it – would pay the price.

Oh, but he was a clever old dog still. He had been slowing the pace for a mile or so and Skreech, aware of linking the line of them, had fallen back from Dog Boy and the others. The dog, Hunger, was nowhere to be seen. The first step north and it had vanished. Red Dog feared he might laugh at the beauty of it all and pressed his hand briefly to his mouth.

Of course, he had noticed for some time that Hunger did not stick as closely to Dog Boy as once he had. The dog seemed to take as much notice of Skreech as of Dog Boy these days. And whenever they were outside, the dog would run over the slightest hill, out of sight. Sometimes, it would bring back a rabbit. Dog? It was more of a wolf really. Wild. That's how it had become his champion; it had a viciousness no other dog could match. But, hah, today was when it had chosen to leave them for good, to sup its own freedom.

Red Dog felt his luck was returning; marvelled that he had been able to add patience to all his other virtues.

Not till today had he found Skreech on his own – always Dog Boy or the old farmer had been around him. But now – *thar she blows*! Red Dog felt a little skip come into his step.

Skreech turned and the skip became an ungainly hobble.

'Keep up,' said Skreech. Skreech, ordering Red Dog! 'My knee, my knee's still not right.'

Skreech looked up ahead. No one in sight.

'Come on.'

Red Dog hirpled till Skreech was within reach. He felt himself flush with pleasure.

Martha saw Red Dog's lips part. He seemed to be making the sound 'S-S-S-S-S' for a long time, his teeth bared, his eyes glinting, the helmet of his forehead closed. But it can only have been for the time it took his hand to travel in an arc across his body, bruising the spring air, before it landed across the side of Martha's head and knocked her off the path between two bushes.

'S-S-Skreech!'

Red Dog had her pinioned. She felt as if she were in a dog kennel as Red Dog's chest and the sides of his coat screened the light from her.

'Oh, Skreech, how I've waited for this.' He slapped her again. Lightly. Playfully.

'Get off me, Red Dog.' Martha wanted to shout, but her chest felt crushed. Her breath was being squeezed from her bit by bit. Red Dog saw the panic in her face.

'Oh, you did the wrong thing, little Skreech, when you betrayed Red Dog. Remember, *once crossed* . . . But now is Red Dog's revenge. For you're coming back with me. You were the cause of my fall, but now you will be my redemption. I'm taking you back to the Invisible

City. The Mount will be happy to have you back. Red Dog shall be redeemed.'

'I'm . . . never . . .'

'Oh, never is such a long time and frankly I don't have time to spare. So save your breath. I can't go back alone, surely you see that. You've got to come and whether I deliver you dead or alive, you'll be a good example for others.'

'I said . . . I'm . . .'

'Oh Skreech,' said Red Dog and his hand reached for a calming rock he had carried for just such an eventuality in his coat's deep pocket.

It was Red Dog's very bad luck that it was his right hand that closed around the rock, because it was from his defenceless right-hand side that Hunger came.

Martha would remember Red Dog's hand instinctively lifting, taking the coat's side with it. She would also recall, below the lifting coat flap, glimpsing Hunger in the air. She had not been able to see the start of his leap, so ever after she would remember, along with Hunger's other attributes, his ability to fly.

Whether Hunger knocked Red Dog clean off Martha or whether Red Dog rolled away from the violence of Hunger's assault, Red Dog found himself on his knees, his right ear torn and bleeding, as Hunger tore at the forearms of the coat he held up to protect his face.

The second Red Dog had left her chest, Martha let out a full cry: 'Bradley!'

They surrounded him now – Bradley, Martha, Victor and Hunger. Floris glared at him from behind one of the bushes. In response to Red Dog's begging, Bradley had signalled Hunger back. But not before he had spread his jaws around Red Dog's face and drawn two neat rows of bleeding beads. Now Hunger paced behind him, like a boxer waiting to see if his opponent would beat the count.

'He was going to kill me,' said Martha.

'Oh, never was I, never was I—'

'To kill me, if I wouldn't go back to The Mount.'

'Oh, nonsense. A story.'

'Shut up, Red Dog. It's over with you.'

'Oh, over, it's over, yes, it's been over a long time. Seven times seven equals what? Eight times five equals what? Oh, two times two equals what? You see how I'm broken. Give a man who's weakened with an attack of nerves another chance. *Satisfaction guaranteed*—'

'Never,' they said together.

'Oh, don't leave me here alone. What's to become of me?'

'Follow us and Hunger will rip your throat out. I swear it,' said Bradley.

'Oh, I am undone. I am undone. How I am undone.'

* * *

They could still hear his cries – 'I am undone' – echoing through the still spring air when they lost sight of him – a gaunt figure in ill-fitting clothes, pleading to the heavens.

In Compound 23, a patrolman sniffed and climbed into an old jeep.

'Vagrants, thieves, mad dogs ... Time we made an end of them all,' he muttered to himself.

CHAPTER 17

THE FOREST

Hunger stayed close to them for the rest of their journey. The farmland was beginning to run into tundra and the firs thickened around the track. They skirted where the water had gathered in the hollows and not yet drained away. In the shadows there was still the occasional edge of ice.

The last night, before they left the Compounds behind them, they spent at the Gilbert farm, knocking three times on the door, repeating, '*What has been lost shall be found. Those who give will have their gifts passed on.*' It had not seemed to calm Mr and Mrs Gilbert.

'The dog?'

'Hunger is with us. If you shelter us, you shelter him.'

They ushered them in, as the Faith demanded. Caught

between the Compounds and the threat of the forest, anxiety seemed to have bled all life from them. Once Mrs Gilbert looked at Floris and said, 'Pretty girl, pretty girl,' chanting the words emptily, her head nodding heavily on the pale stem of her body.

Mr Gilbert brought them blankets and boiled some meal and carrots for them, but he too spoke in the most hushed tones and glanced round nervously at every sound. Bradley was left in no doubt what a weight the Gilberts felt their guests to be.

Yet it was not anxiety that had kept Bradley awake, staring through the skylight at the clusters of stars. Rather it was excitement that the next day they would clear the worlds of the city and the Compounds at last and begin the last stage of their journey.

Just before they left, Mrs Gilbert grasped Bradley's hands in hers. '*What has been lost shall be found. Those who give will have their gifts passed on.* It's true, isn't it?' Her eyes searched Bradley's face, till Martha interrupted.

'We shall pass on your gifts, Mrs Gilbert. So you see it's true.'

'It's true,' Mrs Gilbert said, turning to her husband, tears in her eyes. 'Didn't I tell you, it's true? That everything is still possible.'

And it seemed to Bradley too, as the day developed, after their solemn goodbyes to the Gilberts, that everything was possible. The inside-him world and the outside-him world shared their signs.

A deer leaped before them – in perfect arcs it took to the forest. Hunger saw it as a goad and rushed after it in brief enthusiasm.

An owl passed overhead as they were setting up their shelter for the night with branches and moss. As the owl hooted, Victor sat on his haunches and hooted back. Floris looked at him and laughed. Here, at last, it seemed they had come to a place where they were unafraid to declare themselves. *Hoot-hoot*, Floris went too. *Hoot-hoot*.

In another part of the forest, Claw turned his blind wolf-eyes towards the source of this alien merriment. *Hoot-hoot*, he went and turned back to the wolf folk. He bared his teeth in a grim smile. *Hoot-hoot*.

The track ran out early the following morning. It trickled into a path, trodden by rabbits and deer. The forest turned it into a dark-green corridor, which held them most of the day; so that it came as a shock when darkness ended and light flooded into the wide lake and the sky.

'Look,' said Martha, 'strawberries!'

And there they were, the early spring strawberries, like small coals burning in the greenery.

'Here,' said Bradley, picking a handful quickly, 'taste these.' He held his hand out to Floris and Victor.

They savoured the sweetness of the strawberries and crouched down to pick more for themselves. For Bradley, there was more than a handful of strawberries to savour: there was the growing excitement that their journey was almost at an end. He stood frozen in that moment, and was the first to hear the crack of a twig on the forest floor, as Claw and the two wolf men stepped from behind the curtain of trees.

'Hoot-hoot,' said Claw. 'Hoot-hoot.'

Claw's face was glowing with effort, but also with a certain satisfaction. Though his knee had been on fire and the movement had reawakened an old toothache, he had managed to keep up with the young ones they had shadowed through the forest most of that day. Now he felt his old presence briefly returning to him – the threat of a wolf, the arrogance of a man.

He looked even older than Bradley had thought, when he had seen him from a distance at the lake. His skin was leathery, his chest grey as his thin beard, but his eyes, today at least, were still dark and bright.

Bradley raised his head and coolly sniffed the air, as if there were some foulness in it, some lower form of life. He had left the Old Woman and the life he had known in the Zone. He had faced the treacherous weasel and cruel Red Dog – twice! He had risked all to save Floris from The Mount. And he had almost been broken by his feverish dreams after the storm. Now only the wolf men stood between them and their journey's end. He would not be beaten now.

'If you have come to fight, you have made a mistake. Fight us and my dog will take you first, old man.'

Hunger snarled, his lips lifting, his teeth flashing in the sunlight.

'Not yet, Hunger,' said Martha.

Behind Claw, the two younger men paced as their wolves turned and turned within them. They swung their clubs into their fists. The old man narrowed his eyes and irritably waved the wolf men back.

'Yes,' said Bradley, becoming bolder, 'take your shame back to the forest with you.'

Claw's face hardened. 'You,' he said, 'what do you know? You judge us. You sniff the air like betters. But you're the same. I know the rip-it-up of you, the nose-to-the-bum of you, the fleas-in-the-ears of you.'

'And we,' said Bradley, unflinching, 'we know the fish-breath of you, the scratch-out-the-eyes of you, the bitch-in-heat of you.'

Claw spat on the ground and wiped his hand across his mouth.

Bradley raised his head further and straightened his shoulders.

'Pah,' said Claw, 'we know the kill-the-runt of you,

the brother-fight of you, the shit-in-the-dirt of you. We *smell* the dog in you.'

Claw nodded with finality, as if in agreement with his own challenge. But before Bradley could summon his response, Victor had brushed past him, from where he had been holding Floris, the strawberries now a bloody pulp in her fists, and from where Martha held Hunger and whispered to calm him. Now her other arm reached out around Floris.

Victor uncurled his shoulders and, as Bradley had done, tipped his head back.

'Was a dog, me,' he said. 'Was a dog bit by dogs; the mouths of them on me still.' And he raised his layers of shirt, jersey and top to show his scars.

'But no nose-in-the-dirt dog am I.

'No piss-in-the-bed dog.

'No roll-in-the-muck dog.

'No tear-the-living-flesh dog.

'Now a straight-up am I.

'Now a finger-eater am I.

'Now not only of night am I.

'Victor-with-friends am I.

'Not the same am I.

'Not the same.'

It was the longest Bradley had ever heard him speak. His small cracked voice had the rhythm of a bird stretching forward to defend itself again and again; between times briefly hunching in the silence. But Victor had only met one part of the challenge. For Claw had turned slowly from Bradley during Victor's speech. His eyes seemed fiercer as they bore down into Victor now.

Bradley could see the small blue nerves in Victor's neck tick and his slight sinews strain as he fought to hold his head steady when all his instincts told him to look away. When it appeared he could take no more, Bradley broke into the silence.

'We know your story.'

'Story? What story?' Claw said.

'How you came here from the city, desperate and hungry. You killed wolf and ate wolf and now there is a curse on you. You can be neither man, woman, nor wolf; but nor can you go back to the lives you lived before. Yes, once we were dogs. You sense that in us. But I sense too the straight-up in you, the shame in you, the father in you.'

The old man dipped his head and felt for the wolf-skin draped over his shoulders. He touched it sadly. When he looked up, his black eyes were clouded. He spread his arms wide; in the same gesture he had offered Red Dog at the lake.

'Oh, no need for the wolf talk now,' he said. 'We have worn all that long enough. The father in you never dies, boy. Whether you are dog or man – or my old familiar, the wolf – the father in you will not die. You will learn that sometime for yourself.

'I left my family in the city at the Dead Time. I came here and I found food, plentiful food. I told myself, my wife and my son were better off without me; there were others who could take care of them better. But all of us who ate wolf had a price to pay.

'I never understood where my pain lay – the wolf inside me or the loss of my child gnawing at me. I have fathered again and again, but it seems each child I father is replaced by the dying child I left in that city all these years ago and I find myself again howling at the moon.'

He turned and waved and out of the forest came the two women, the baby and one of the boys. They dragged forward a rough wooden stretcher on which lay the other boy, pale and fevered, whom Red Dog had struck.

'Another one,' the old man said, 'see how the curse goes on.'

He stepped forward and put his clawed, arthritic hand on Bradley's shoulder.

'No, my boy, you do not know our story. For you cannot wear our story, you cannot know what it feels like to have your story live within you. To know that the one feeling that tells you you're alive is your pain. Look at me, boy. Look – at your story wolf.'

Bradley did as he was asked. He looked for what felt a long time at the bow-legged old man with the mangy headdress; at his scars, at his swollen knuckles and at his still, stony face.

'I heard a call. I had hoped . . . for I don't know what. Come,' Claw said, turning to the wolf folk, 'we have no enemy here, nor anyone who can help us.'

With enormous slowness, as if their feet were weighed down with rocks, led by Claw, they lifted the branches of the stretcher, turned, and melted back into the forest's depths.

Victor dropped to his haunches and took a few heaving breaths. Floris quickly picked more strawberries, thinking their sweetness might revive him. Bradley left them to it. He hurried further round the bay towards the thick overhanging bush whose poisonous berries shone invitingly in the late afternoon light.

He bent over and, grasping a branch, pulled it up. In its empty shadow the black waters glistened. Bradley let it fall.

Disappointment was like a stone on his chest. He heaved in air and breathed it out as if all his hopes went with it. From where he crouched, ripping handfuls of grass, he turned to find Martha behind him.

'Maybe . . .' she began.

'. . . I've been stupid,' Bradley finished.

Floris and Victor had come over now, sensing the despairing mood; their stained hands hung by their sides around a mess of strawberries.

'I'm sorry,' said Bradley.

They looked, one to the other, in acknowledgement of how far they had come, how hard they had tried, how pointless and lonely it all seemed now.

But one of the company was not so despondent. Hunger was poised and alert. He was leaning towards the heart of the lake, his eyes flaming yellow in the slanted sunlight, his ears pricked.

His senses were focused with such intensity on something 'out there' that the others were soon drawn towards his field of concern.

But all they could see were the wind-ruffled waters of the lake and the small, dark island. As they watched, two blue herons returned across the waters to roost. Then again, nothing but the wind, stronger than before.

Hunger never moved.

Till Bradley whispered, 'There. See. Left of the island.'

'Yes, something,' said Martha. 'A boat, it must be a boat.'

Hunger began to pace, to look as if he might simply launch himself into the lake. Victor too went one way, then the other, as if a better angle might clarify what it was they were watching.

It was a boat, a small boat, but it had a mast and a full black sail. Was this the ship of death come for them? If so, Hunger was very eager to be first to board it. For now, he began to bark towards the boat, his eyes aflame with excitement.

And it came back. Softly certainly, but clearly and unmistakably, an answering bark.

'Shelter.' It was Floris's first word after the months of silence. 'Shelter.'

They could see Shelter now at the prow of the boat, her paws on the edge of it, barking her greeting to each of them. And they could see that, instead of a mast and a full sail, the Old Woman stood there – seven feet tall, arms outstretched – with the wind filling out her black cloak.

In her excitement, Floris took her blue glass and flung it as far as she could into the lake. For a moment it hung in the air and the last fierce light coming from the sky and from the water kissed it a brilliant blue.

They never saw the Old Woman working that miracle again. 'Extraordinary times give rise to extraordinary attributes,' she said, adding, 'as I'm sure you're only too well aware.' In fact, when Bradley described Red Dog and his helmet frown to her, she recalled a bank manager she had once known – a rather small man, bald as an egg, who had loved amateur dramatics. She herself had never cared for him. 'Pompous little man at heart.'

'Do you really think . . . ?' said Bradley.

'Unlikely, most unlikely. Still, you never know . . .'

She had her own story to tell, of course, of how Shelter and she had set out for the cabin the morning after Bradley and Hunger had left. As a blind old beggar woman, shrunk inside her cloak, with only a dog to guide her, she had been threatened once or twice and been mocked by boy soldiers and vagrants, but anyone could see she was not worth robbing and let her go on her way. They had just made it to the cabin before the heavy snows came. Old stocks of tinned food and the occasional rabbit or fish had seen them through the winter and there were lots of warm clothes in a trunk the mice had not got at. Now they were working to clear a vegetable garden and a flower garden.

'Flowers!' said Floris.

'Yes,' said the Old Woman. 'I have plans to live in ordinary times.'

'Plans?' said Bradley.

'It's what you do if you believe in the future.'

Part of the Old Woman's plans involve daily lessons in reading and writing. She insists now on being called Mrs Newton – though out of class Bridget is perfectly acceptable.

At night she reads to them from the old shelf of yellowing, broken-backed books in the cabin – *White Fang*, *Oliver Twist*, *Peter Pan*. Soon she can share the reading with Martha – and, for short spells, Bradley –

though Victor will occasionally grab a book from their grasp, finding something so striking he pores over the page, as if words are animals that might leave a spoor behind them.

'It's only the words,' says Mrs Newton. 'Only words and your imagination.'

Victor looks at her suspiciously. Of all her pupils he needs the most reassurance. He resents the way Floris has begun to follow Bridget around, to obviously enjoy laying her head on Bridget's lap as she reads. So Bridget values those moments when Victor comes near, when he looks intently at the page and stays beside Floris, as she reads on. Soon she will lay a hand on Victor's head and he will not shake it off.

And in the summer sunlight, on the edge of the lake, Victor straightens. Next year he will not be too shy to take off his shirt and let the sun soothe his scars. Then he will pick for golden-haired Floris the first bunch of flowers.

Martha's hair too has grown long and shiny – it reminds Bradley of the colour of spring strawberries. Without the constraints she had willed upon it, her body loses its boyishness.

She swims through the lake like a fish. There is a small island which she and Bradley like to race to. Most often, Martha wins. She waits at its edge, kicking her smooth calves in the water – looking at Bradley with fresh, laughing eyes.

In the evening, after the readings, there are other stories by the stove.

The Old Woman, for again it is she, tells them that there is a world out there, waiting; that soon it will change again, for the better, and that sometime they could play a part in helping it on its way.

Bradley sees Chloe's face in the lamplight. He can summon her image any time he wants now; and the face also of their old neighbour, Margaret, who used to take him in from the leaking house and offer him a bowl of broth.

Even so, the Old Woman says, they must remember.

'What is the world made of?'

'Ashes. Dust.'

'All worlds. But what cannot crumble? What cannot be burnt or be broken?'

'Stories.'

'Stories,' she says. Then, with a smile, 'Now be gone and let an old woman get some sleep.'

Bradley lies in his bunk and listens. Each night, as the sun turns red and sinks below the black line of firs, he hears their singing. It is a tapestry of cries and of howls. Yet still he can pick out the thread of Hunger's voice in this, his last season, as he sings to them and to Shelter.

Shelter will not join his pack, but her pups – his pups – will. The forest will be theirs again and whoever comes there will have to find a way of living with them.

ABOUT THE AUTHOR

Tom Pow is the award-winning author of four books of poetry – *Rough Seas*, *The Moth Trap*, *Red Letter Day* and *Landscapes and Legacies*. He has also written three radio plays, a travel book about Peru – *In the Palace of Serpents* – and three picture books – *Who Is the World For?*, *Callum's Big Day* and *Tell Me One Thing, Dad*. *Scabbit Isle*, published in 2003 by CORGI BOOKS was his first novel for young adults.

Tom Pow was Writer in Residence at the Edinburgh International Book Festival from 2001 till 2003. He works at Glasgow University Crichton Campus in Dumfries, where he teaches courses in creative writing and storytelling.